Honor and Grace
Book Three Poore Pond School Trilogy

Ruth Harwell Fawcett

Cover Artist: Pamela Dills

Ambrosia Press
Cleveland

OTHER BOOKS BY RUTH FAWCETT

Honor in the Heart
A Novel

Honor Me Honor You
Poore Pond Series Book Two

HONOR and GRACE
Book Three Poore Pond School Trilogy

Published by Ambrosia Press LLC

Printed in the United States of America. For information address:
Ambrosia Press LLC, 2 Waban Road, Willow House, Timberlake, Ohio 44095-1952
www.ruthfawcettbooks.com

Paperback ISBN-13: 978-0-9778656-7-3   Hardcover ISBN-13: 978-0-9778656-6-6

FIRST EDITION

Acknowledgments

I am indebted to loyal readers who have patiently awaited this final book in the trilogy and have encouraged me with their kind inquiries as to its progress.

I thank my husband Bill for his constant support of my writing and the clever way in which he works it into conversations at every opportunity.

Cover artist, Pamela Dills, has once again fashioned a cover that is meaningful to the story and reflects her special talent for creating beautiful, painterly scenes that draw in the reader. I greatly appreciate her talent, quick grasp of ideas, and reliability.

I thank Bob Dills for his support and generosity as liaison to the printer.

I owe a great debt to Elliot D. Tiller for his willing and thorough advice on certain legal scenes important to the plot of this book.

Readers Arlene Fenton and Roberta Smearman provided consistency for the trilogy by providing valuable feedback throughout, and they have my thanks.

Teri and Chuck Hare at Rabbit Enterprises — always congenial — provided further consistency for the trilogy with their skilled graphics work and Teri's exceptional eye for design.

Thanks to Tom Dorow and Syndi Barber at Cushing-Malloy for their compatibility and for seeing to the consistent and quality printing of all three novels in the Poore Pond trilogy.

Dedication

To my extraordinary great grandchildren: Henley and Mary Addington Ingram, Savannah and Jon Paul Gray, all under four years of age, who, as children of teachers, have a head start on the world of words and—in our family—the world of wordplay.

To committed teachers everywhere: you know that there is no substitute for the likes of you when it comes to making a difference in the lives of our children.

To the memory of Adam Dills,
a bright presence who left us far too early.

Chapter One
Hope

Hope rolled over, pulling the cotton blanket around her ears.

The sound came again.

She buried her head in the pillow.

Again, the sound came.

She raised her shoulders to rest on her elbows and barely managed to pry open her eyes. The sound came again, more loudly than before; and then she knew she had not been dreaming. Someone was knocking at her door.

The oversized numerals on the bedside clock shouted the time: 4:24 A.M.

Her first thought was of George. Yes, he was an adult; but he was still her son. Something's happened.

Hope rushed toward the stairs, slipping into her silk robe as she ran. The knocking grew louder and more fervent.

Heart racing, she ran to the front door and switched on the outside light as she peered through the peephole. She saw the square face and coarse blonde hair of a man who seemed somewhat familiar. She could not quite place him.

She felt his impatience through the thick, carved-oak door but could not bring herself to open it.

"Hope! Hope!" the man shouted. "Open the door! It's Mark; you know me, Michael's kid brother. Open the door."

Buoyed by relief that this had nothing to do with her George, she quickly slid open the chain and turned the deadbolt. Hesitating just long enough to shrug off a feeling of dread, she opened the door.

They shared an awkward near-hug before he turned to wave away the taxi. His hair and clothes reeked of cigarette smoke.

"Come in, Mark. Come in," she said, stepping aside to let him enter first.

He bent to pick up a small piece of hard-sided luggage. Hope's eyes shot right to the frayed cuffs on his dark blazer. He stepped into the foyer.

Old memories began spinning in her mind. A feeling of dread returned and intensified. Questions clustered in her throat. Why are you here? How long has it been since you've seen Michael? Why did you come to me and not to him? And why have you come at this wicked hour?

She watched Mark repeatedly brush back his hair with his hand, shifting his weight from one foot to the other.

"Do you have coffee, Hope?" he asked, his voice and body oozing agitation.

"Of course," she countered. "Come with me to the kitchen." She led him toward the hallway.

'This is a nice place, Hope. How long have you and Michael lived here?" He walked to the windows and peered into the shadowy back yard.

Had it been that long? Hope felt sure that Mark had attended their wedding. But she and Michael had lived together in this house for sixteen years—until the separation. Had they never invited Mark here? Has he forgotten about their divorce?

Hope put coffee on to brew while Mark stood silently at the window. His unspoken explanation hung heavily over the room. She laid the table with tapestry placemats and linen napkins, cups, saucers, spoons, sugar, and cream. She put on a kettle of water and placed a teabag at her place.

Their utter silence filled the room with tension. She rummaged in cupboards and the pantry for some sort of quick, suitable snack, finally choosing chocolate biscotti from a large tin. I hope it's not too terribly stale, she thought as she placed it on a clean plate, wondering how long she had had it.

The coffeemaker beeped.

"Mark, let's sit down," she called softly.

The kettle began to whistle. "Mark, coffee's ready," she called again, pouring hot water over a teabag.

"Mark!" she said in raised voice, pouring steaming coffee into his cup. "Please sit down!"

He joined her at the table and drank the coffee black, savoring it as if it were the last he would ever have.

They sat in silence, looking at each other over their cups.

Finally, Hope could bear it no longer. "Mark, what on earth brings you here after all these years? And why at this ungodly hour? Why have you come to me and not to Michael? What's going on?"

He spread his graceful hands on the table; they were trembling. Hope's apprehension rose.

"Isn't Michael here?" he asked, eyes scanning the doorways.

Her voice even, she told him about the divorce and how bitter it all was, about George's dropping out of college and living on the street for four years. Her eyes filled when she told him how painful it was not to know how or where her only child lived.

When Mark reached across the table and laid his hand on hers, she saw the emotion in his eyes. "I'm so sorry, Hope. I thought you and Michael had reconciled. That's what he told me—at one point—." His voice trailed off and he looked away.

"But things are much better now." She withdrew her hand and gave a mechanical smile. "George finally came home. He's become a wonderful young man with a very giving heart, and he and his father are close again. In fact, George works with Michael at PolyFlem."

Confusion covered his face.

"You don't know about PolyFlem, do you?" Hope said.

He squinted and shook his head.

"It's a polymer company Michael started two years ago. He seems to be growing the company well; it's international now, I know that much." She smiled at him. "You can be proud of your big brother at last."

"I've always been proud of my brother, Hope." Mark said quite forcefully. "We've been out of touch too many years, but he was always there for me when I needed him."

Hope tried to mask her surprise. Surprise turned into shock when he told her that Michael had paid his way through law school after their father died with no assets.

"He didn't have a regular income then either. But he had all those deals going; he worked eighteen-hour days, juggling it all." Mark's face lit up with pride in the telling.

"He set me up in a small law office, too." He dropped his eyes.

"Has that been successful for you?" she asked, her eyes seeking his.

"I made a decent living. Until I got sick, that is." He looked away. "Now all I can do are wills and business documents."

Hope's head churned with these disclosures. It sounded to her as if Mark were talking about another Michael. The Michael she had married and divorced was angry, selfish, critical.

"Tell me about your sickness, Mark." She looked at him with soft eyes.

When he told her he was on dialysis and urgently needed a kidney transplant, she knew why he had come.

Emotionally spent, Hope made him comfortable in George's old room and crawled into her cold bed though dawn was just beginning to break.

She no longer felt resentment toward Mark; a list of heart-wrenching concerns formed in her mind. Obviously, if Michael weren't a match to be a donor for Mark, George might be in line as a possible match. She would not think about that.

The news that loathsome Michael had done noble deeds stunned her; it unsettled her terribly. She did not know whether to embrace the notion for what it had meant to Mark and could mean to George. Or should she go on despising him for the miserable husband he had been to her?

~ ~ ~

Hope slept fitfully for about an hour and then awoke. Though it was mid-July and she still had two weeks of summer break, she was unable to stay in bed. Mark's presence just down the hall dominated her thoughts. He will have to connect with Michael as soon as possible, she said to herself, rising tiredly from the bed.

She slipped into a modest cotton robe and tied the belt securely. She and George would be meeting tonight with the Board of Directors and Theo to address, once and for all, the issue of protesting neighbors at the homeless shelter. She really wanted to focus on that single mission today.

She passed Mark's room, seeing through the open door, his still figure under the blankets. She went downstairs.

Determining how to pacify the protestors was overwhelming enough, but she found the thought of facing Theo again after his abrupt coolness toward her a month ago even more troubling.

She put on a fresh pot of coffee and water for tea.

Her mind flashed back to their last evening together, a Friday night after two arduous weeks of closing school. They were having a lovely dinner at their favorite restaurant. Warmth flowed between them like a delicious spring breeze. Feeling wonderfully blessed and safe, she had unloaded on him all the predicaments she had dealt with recently.

She described the gut-wrenching situation of Phyllis Meadow's having been charged with child endangering of her lovely daughter and how the family had moved away in the night.

She spoke of Ian Bradford, father of five, who turned to illegal deals for extra family income. In her view, he was being unfairly prosecuted for just trying to take care of his family.

In a rare moment, she had dropped her guard and disclosed her own fear that she could be ultimately prosecuted as an embezzler.

She would never forget the way he had looked at her with clear distaste after she told him she had deceptively—*fraudulently* was the word she had used—acquired money a long time ago, when she was very young. She knew at once that she had made a grave mistake in sharing her dirty little secret with him.

The egg cooker, seldom used, was at the back of a lower cupboard; she kneeled to move pots and bowls from in front of it, stirring musty odors to the forefront.

Theo had avoided her on all sides ever since that night. As consultant for the foundation she and George had formed to fund a homeless shelter they were running, he needed to convey necessary information at times. He dutifully kept her informed but restricted messages to email and text messages. There had been no more warm phone calls, no more personal meetings or dinners.

She filled the egg cooker's reservoir with water but waited to put the plug in the outlet, wondering whether to let Mark sleep or to wake him.

Over and over, she had analyzed every word between Theo and her that night, trying to understand. She had come up short every time.

She set the table and put multi-grain bread slices in the toaster without activating it, savoring the comforting smell of life-giving bread.

It struck her now that the three worrisome situations she had described to Theo that night had one thing in common: law enforcement was a factor in each one.

Of course, that's it. Poor straight Theo has had no experience with the legal system. A man like him obviously has never broken a law in his life. Hope shuddered at the shock he must have gone through, hearing of such dishonorable situations in connection with her, and from her very lips. She was the woman whose company he had enjoyed immensely, with whom he had everything in common, and with whom he was on the verge of a serious romance.

Hope heard movement and water running upstairs. She finalized the breakfast preparations and was just peeling six-minute eggs when Mark appeared. Though still tired around the eyes, he looked rested and fresh in clean khakis and plaid shirt.

"Good morning, Mark," she said, motioning him to sit at the table.

"Good morning, Hope." His brow furrowed slightly. "You've gone to a lot of trouble for me, and I haven't much time."

"I know, Mark. I wanted you to have a good breakfast before you called Michael." She poured his coffee and served his eggs and toast.

"I've already spoken to him," he said. "He's picking me up in twenty minutes."

Mark hurried through breakfast and waited outside for Michael. Hope did not protest; she had no desire to face her ex-husband when she had pressing problems to sort.

Anxiety niggled at her as she cleared the breakfast dishes. She closed the dishwasher, dried her hands, and went to the computer in her study. The light of dawn filled the room when she opened the curtains.

> Good morning, Theo, she typed. Are you free to speak privately with me before the board meeting tonight? If it's agreeable to you, I will arrive 30 minutes early, just long enough for us to clear the air a bit for a better working relationship. Please advise.
> Hope.

Without stopping to proofread, she quickly clicked the send button.

Hope, undressing, searched her mind for words to use with Theo. Stepping into a hot shower, she tried to sort her racing thoughts. "Theo, I know you have no patience with losers, certainly not with felons [No. No, too harsh]. Theo, desperate people often do desperate things. Haven't you ever been desperate? [No. That's putting my issue back on him]"

She turned the water hotter to rinse her lathered body, hotter still to wash away her sins. Soothed by melon-scented body wash, she prayed softly for the right words. A cold-water rinse brought her back to the moment.

~ ~ ~

George dropped in unexpectedly for lunch, bringing vegetarian wraps for them both and waffle fries for himself. He found his mother at her desk, listing ideas for calming militant neighbors at the shelter.

He led her and her list to the kitchen table where he served their sandwiches on small plates.

"What about Uncle Mark, Mom?" George asked before either of them took a bite. "He looks good, doesn't he?"

"Well, yes he does, considering —" She wondered where Mark was having lunch. Probably at Michael's favorite pub.

"A little older but still fit," George interrupted.

She picked up the list. "Help me with this, George. You know we have the meeting tonight."

"Oh no, I forgot about the meeting," he said, slapping his forehead. "I agreed to play handball with Uncle Mark. He looked away. "Well, we'll just have to go earlier, before the meeting."

"Do you think a fence around the building, an ornamental fence, of course, but still a fence, would make the neighbors feel better?"

"You mean as in *Good fences make good neighbors,* Mom?" George said.

"Sort of, yes. Not so much to fence the neighbors out but more to be seen as fencing the residents inside."

"You mean a psychological barrier, don't you?"

"Of course." She furrowed her brow. "But then a fence is a big expenditure, isn't it?"

They brainstormed a list of possible reasons the shelter might be making the neighbors uncomfortable. George mentioned the Metro bus stop in front of the building where the residents waited for buses, sometimes as many as six or eight of them at a time.

"You're right. Anytime they move about in numbers they attract attention," Hope agreed. "That's what happens on Saturday when so many non-residents come to the Open Breakfast."

"Oh, that Sadie woman with the flaming red hair and purple feather boa could be the poster child for misfits," George laughed. "And she never misses a breakfast. Nice human being, though. She's always helping people, carries a can-opener, plastic bags, a box of wipes—you name it—in her bag and shares them with everyone."

"Who's that small man with the tweed overcoat and the limp who always has a trail of dogs following him?" she asked.

"You mean Clarence. He carries bits of meat in his pockets and feeds every stray animal he sees on the street. He gets a big kick out of it."

"A.J. is working with him, isn't he, George?" she asked.

"A.J. may have phased him out. I'm not sure." George said, taking the last bite of his wrap. He stood and gathered oily plates and napkins from the table.

"I have to go back to work, Mom." He leaned and kissed her cheek. "Is Theo picking you up for the meeting?"

"No, I'm on my own tonight." She did not look at him. "Good-bye, dear."

Why haven't I told him that Theo and I have had a falling out? Is that what we call it? What is it really? A total disconnect.

She thought of other high-profile acts the residents or guests might do outside the building and added a few more ideas to the list.

Theo's email reply dismayed her:

> A private pre-meeting between you and me
> would be entirely inappropriate, Hope. It would
> be seen by the Board as secretive and
> underhanded.
> Theo.

President Warren Gray opened the George Fleming Foundation Board of Trustees' meeting by welcoming everyone and stating the purpose of the special meeting.

Hope and Theo sat on the same side but at opposite ends of the rectangular table. Having arrived after Theo did, Hope chose her seat so as not to face him. When she came in, she had called a collective greeting to all at the table and managed to send fleeting eye contact his way. He looked her way but not at her.

Every member seemed to have an idea, and they ran the gamut from ignoring the demonstrations altogether to meeting with the protesters to try to win them over.

After Hope shared her and George's ideas for lowering the visibility of the people they served, Theo voiced his agreement and added another. "Would it help to stagger their hours of unscheduled time so that they came and went individually rather than in pairs or groups?"

"But, Theo, we don't want to make them feel that they have no control of their personal time," George interjected. "They may be near the bottom of the food chain, so to speak; but they are still entitled to their dignity."

Hope listened to their polite dialogue, admiring George's passion and enjoying Theo's rich voice. She found herself longing for the old relationship she'd had with him.

"We are running a shelter, not a prison," Brooke announced. The word *shelter* implies protection." She looked intently from one person to the next, and they all looked back at her. "And if their sense of dignity is not preserved, it won't matter how well we meet any of their other needs. They won't grow from our services."

Hope, caught up in Brooke's charisma, had forgotten that the professional staff was invited to the meeting. Reminded of Michael's relationship with her, she tried once again—but was unable to visualize the elegant Brooke and crusty Michael as a couple.

Then she remembered Mark's account of the many ways Michael had helped him, and her image of the caring social worker attracted to the benevolent elder brother became more believable.

To close the meeting, Warren Gray pounded the gavel, bringing Hope back to the moment. He began a terse summary of strategies the group had identified. The Board will:

- Stagger arrival and departure times of residents, avoiding groups but allowing pairs so as to meet their social needs.

- Look into assigning a role model in shirt and tie to supervise bus-stop behavior during peak times (Milan? Or volunteer?).

- Seek cost estimates of fencing, both wrought iron and resin materials to allow price comparison.

- Coach Clarence in the importance of being a good neighbor, and require him to stop carrying meat or otherwise inviting dogs.

- Remind Open Breakfast guests of basic good-neighbor behavior.

- Invite all neighbors to a town-hall type meeting where they may voice their opinions and help identify solutions. Instill in them, a sense of the noble purpose the shelter serves and invite volunteers to help at the shelter.

The meeting closed and Hope walked out with George. Theo approached them and walked alongside her. "I trust you understood my response to your email, Hope," he began, not looking at her.

"Perfectly," she said, stealing a sidelong glance at his face.

"Anybody interested in ice cream or milk shakes?" George asked, leaning forward to look at Theo.

For a moment, no one spoke. Then Hope clipped, "Count me out. It's late."

"Perhaps another time, George," Theo said, seeking Hope's unreceptive eyes. "Well, goodnight, colleagues." He headed off toward the other side of the parking lot.

George walked his mother to her car and said goodbye with a warm hug. "You and Theo will get it back, Mom. Don't fret," he said softly into her ear.

Chapter Two
Ray

Ray hoisted two bulky boxes onto the dumb waiter and pulled the lever, sending it up to the second floor. He wiped sweat from his brow with a damp handkerchief, grabbed a plastic bag filled with small rolls of carpet, and headed toward the stairs.

Bluewave Stonecipher was on a stepladder, attaching a banner to the wall above the door. *It's there inside you,* the watery blue banner read, the words floating on ocean waves.

He artfully twisted both his body and the bag around the ladder.

"Just put that bag on the round table, please, Ray," she said.

"My, it is warm today, isn't it?" She pinched the sides of her blouse and fanned them.

"There's a floor fan in the storage room, Bluewave. I'll get it for you." Ray started toward the door.

"Never mind, Ray," she said, brushing flowing hair from her face. "It's too powerful, blows all my papers and things out of place." She laughed. "I'll be fine as soon as I open the window to get the cross ventilation from your attic fan."

Ray had the window opposite the door opened before she could descend the ladder.

"Thanks, Ray. You are such a help. Have a bit of juneberry tea," she said, motioning her elbow toward a thermos next to a stack of four-ounce paper cups. "It stimulates the body's natural cooling abilities." She climbed down the ladder.

"No thanks, I'm fine, Bluewave. I have a power drink going downstairs."

Her eyes studied the banner. "Does that look straight to you, Ray?" She stepped back to stare at it.

"It's a little lower on the left," Ray said, instantly climbing the ladder and adjusting the corner. "How's that?" He turned toward her.

"That's better. Thank you." As he descended the ladder, she handed him a packet of teabags. "Have these for later, Ray, and take some to Heather. They can be soothing when you're not feeling quite yourself."

Ray did not want to talk about Heather's condition. He was still trying to understand what multiple sclerosis was and how he could help his fiancée stay well. "What does that mean anyway, that saying on your banner?" he asked, slipping the packet into his shirt pocket, managing a small smile.

She looked up at the banner. "*It's there inside you?*" She faced him with wide eyes. "That's my entire teaching philosophy, Ray." She brushed packing-paper bits off her long, floating, blue-patterned skirt then returned her eyes to his. "I don't ever lose sight of it. It shapes the way I help the class approach everything they do, every problem they solve. Learning problems, social problems, body problems, mood problems, you name it."

Ray rubbed his raised chin and stared at the words. Finally, he asked, "How does it work?" He squinted his eyes.

"Just think about it, Ray." She raised her eyebrows and stared at him.

"Can you give me an example?" He laughed.

"Give it some thought and get back to me. Then I'll give you examples if you haven't gotten it yet."

Ray went back to classroom B-4 to see if the floor had dried, so he could apply another coat of wax. Bluewave's words pestered him endlessly. *It's there inside you.*

Ray applied wax to the classroom floor, finding it unusually difficult to spread and wondered whether the extreme August heat was the cause. Heck, I wax all these floors every August, and it's always hot, he thought. When he reached the last few inches in the wax bucket, spreading was even more difficult. He stopped.

~ ~ ~

Ray climbed into the van with a complimentary new two-gallon can of floor wax. Bud Snipes at Business Chemicals told him that he'd had an entire shipment of bad wax. Dozens of customers had come to complain about the same problem Ray had: poorly spreading, sticky consistency. The Chinese manufacturer admitted to Bud that a disgruntled employee had deliberately left out a prime ingredient that affected the viscosity of the solution. Bud's office was sending out electronic recall messages.

"Now I have to remove all that bad wax," Ray said to himself as he pulled onto the highway. "Good thing I stopped before the room was even one-quarter done." But it did not matter now.

He could hardly contain his excitement. Hope had suggested he pick up the wax and then visit Heather with a take-out lunch, not to worry too much about the time.

Heather, face flushed and smiling, opened the door for him. She was dressed in a tight, black unitard and short socks. The soothing voice of her yoga instructor came from the television.

"Hi, Heather," Ray said, hugging her too tightly. "Are you not finished with your yoga yet?"

"Oh, I finished ten minutes ago, Ray." She motioned for him to sit at the table where there were two straw placemats and sunflower-patterned napkins. "I was just starting over again to fill the time until you came. I figured it wouldn't hurt me to do a little extra."

"How are you feeling today, Heather-soon-to-be-Sellers?"

"I'm fine, Ray Sellers," she said, smiling.

Ray washed his hands at the sink and opened the food bag. He placed small salads and a pack of breadsticks at their places. Heather poured two glasses of lemonade and put out a saucer of oatmeal cookies.

They sat savoring the food and each other, toes touching under the table.

"Have you thought anymore about a wedding date?" Ray locked his eyes with hers.

"I think about it all the time, Ray," she said, her voice heartrending.

"We could still do it in October, Ther-sell," he said using the name he had coined by combining parts of her first and his last. "I know you wanted to be married in the fall." He said, shameless lovesickness in his voice and face. He took her hand across the table. "This is only August. We could put a nice little home wedding together by October. Claire and Aunt Peggy would love to help."

"I don't know, Ray." Heather rose from the table and began clearing the remains of their meal.

"You don't know if you want to marry me? Are you getting cold feet, Heather?" he asked, his voice deliberately light.

She folded her arms around him. "I want that more than anything," she said breathlessly. They held the embrace for several seconds. She broke away first.

"I just have to sort out all this MS stuff, you know, Ray. I have to feel I have a handle on it." She threw the lunch debris in the trash.

"I thought we were doing that, with the yoga and healthful eating, the medicine, your counselor." He looked away. "I thought it was sorted out."

"Just give me a little more time, Ray, please. You've been more than patient. Can you be patient just a tiny bit longer?" She said to his back.

He turned toward her. "I have to get to work, Heather."

Ray drove too fast back to Poore Pond School. A rush of feelings flooded over him; he felt hurt, resentful, frightened, disappointed, and helpless. It was all he could do to keep from turning around and returning to Heather to have it out with her. But thoughts of the mood swings and depression described in the brochure on multiple sclerosis kept him from it. He had promised himself to give her complete emotional support, and he would.

Chapter Three
The Bradfords

Helsi sat at the kitchen table, surrounded by a legal pad and piles of bills. She scrutinized the credit-card statement, item by item. The eight hundred dollars in court costs and fines was down to a six-hundred-dollar balance.

She sat back in her chair and rubbed her temples. We should have that paid off in three months at the latest, she thought. If I can pick up two more cleaning contracts, we'll pay it off sooner.

She went to the phone and dialed the voice-mail number, hoping one of the managers who had seemed interested in Helsi's Cleaning Service had left a confirmation. No new messages.

She sat down again and opened the business checkbook. The $2100 balance shone up at her, making her at once proud of her income and fearful that it would not cover the outstanding household accounts and Ian's fifty-dollar payment to his probation officer next week, twenty-two dollars to his counselor the following Tuesday.

She made a mental note to transfer a thousand dollars to their personal checking account, resenting the fact that she had to keep proper business records for her LLC company. It would be much easier and quicker to just deposit earnings into their personal account. She wrote a company check to herself, filled out a deposit slip for the other account, then wrote a one-hundred dollar check to Ian.

Hearing his car in the drive, she stuffed the checks into her purse and swept away the bills and budget list to a drawer in the laundry room. She dusted her hands and stepped into the kitchen just as he came through the door.

"Hi hon," she called, willing cheer into her voice. "How was class?"

"You won't believe how boring it was, Helsi," Ian said, placing his canvas briefcase on a chair. They hugged briefly.

"All the state regulations on safety in a medical office —I mean, there are rules covering every possible area." He spread his hands for emphasis. "We are learning about safety to the nth degree: *bloodborne pathogens, asbestos awareness*—even something called *confined space entry* . Next week it's *ergonomics*." He threw up his palms in frustration.

Helsi gestured to her husband to sit at the table. "What is *ergonomics,* Ian?" She filled a cup from the coffee maker and brought it to him, along with a pack of cheese crackers from the children's snack drawer. "I know it has something to do with *carpal tunnel* that I'm always threatening to come down with now that I spend so much time on the computer."

"Right, hon," he said. "*Ergonomics* is all about people's efficiency in the workplace. It's meant to avoid stress or injury; such as the carpal tunnel syndrome you are determined to develop." They exchanged smiles.

Helsi looked at the clock and stood. "It's ten forty-five, Ian. I need to leave."

"It's Wednesday, Helsi. You don't go to Heather Baker's on Wednesday, do you?" Ian stood with her.

"No, I don't. But I wanted to stop and see how she's doing. There's a two-story office building near her apartment that I'm trying to contract." She opened the refrigerator and pointed to a tuna pasta salad.

"Oh, that reminds me," he interjected. "Dr. Fleming called to talk to you about whether Heather might need you for more hours now that she's been diagnosed with multiple sclerosis."

"Did you tell her I have no more hours to give? Helsi asked, exasperation in her voice. Ian did not respond.

"The pasta salad, that's for lunch, Ian."

"So what are you saying? You're going to make a sales call over there, too?" He looked at her neat cotton skirt and shape-flattering tee as if only just noticing them.

"That's right, Ian." She touched his arm. "What?"

"It would be nice if we could have lunch together. I just came home, and now you're off." He dropped his eyes. "Then you'll leave right after dinner and go clean offices." He walked to the window and stared out.

What is he talking about? He knows we have to get through this probation and everything, she told herself.

"Oh, Ian." She put her hand around his waist, feeling the tension in his body. "You know this is temporary until we get through the probation and you go back to work at the fire station."

"But is it, Helsi?" He looked at her with cold eyes.

"Is it what, Ian?"

"Is it really temporary?" He looked away. "You seem to be enjoying it all so much." His voice dropped.

"Don't be silly." She put her hands on his shoulder and turned him toward her. "What I am enjoying is helping keep this family going. Paying the bills. Helping you get through a traumatic time." He turned away and she turned with him. "Being supportive," she said in his face.

He shook his head as if to shake her away and asked, "What time do the kids get back from their summer rec program?"

"In about forty-five minutes. Just give them their lunch; they like that pasta salad. Give them fruit and cookies for dessert, and they will be fine," she said, grabbing her purse.

She rushed out the door.

Ian began setting the table for lunch. But he could not get his mind off Helsi. She looked so good in her business clothes. She deals mostly with men, too, I just bet. And her confidence—her confidence is way up there. Heck! That makes her even more attractive.

Why don't I just chuck it all and stay home, let Helsi earn the income? He continued to feed the beast in him. I'd be a heck of a Mr. Mom; I know it. He filled glasses with ice water, rebelliously using his wife's best tall glasses. As if to prove his point, he cut wedges of watermelon and arranged them on a white china platter, finishing just as the children burst through the door.

Ian was quiet at the lunch table, but the children hardly noticed. They were discussing their field trip to the chocolate factory, and each child stated his opinions.

Rachel placed her souvenir chocolate-covered cookie treat next to her plate with great ceremony. Robbie and Dylan looked enviously at it, regretting having eaten their own on the bus.

"What's for dessert, Dad? Robbie asked. "Dad?"

Ian blinked and looked at the boy. "Dessert? That's what the watermelon is, Robbie. It's for dessert."

Rachel made much of unwrapping her cookie slowly and carefully, her face smug and superior.

"May we eat ours outside, Dad?" Dylan asked, already on his feet.

"Sure," Ian said. "But where are Sean and Lucy?"

"They had to stay for a planning meeting. They're figuring out what we're doing next year," Robbie said.

"Dad, you know Sean and Lucy are Summer Recreation Counselors, don't you?" Rachel asked in her authoritative voice.

"Oh, that's right. I forgot," Ian muttered.

~ ~ ~

Trapped in unusually heavy traffic, Helsi kept thinking of Ian. I know he's having a rough time adjusting to all this, she worried. He's such a proud man. And his sense of manliness can be fragile anyway, even more so now.

"But I'm only doing what I have to do," she said aloud as she pulled into Heather's driveway. "So I happen to be enjoying it. What's so terrible about that?" This glib attitude did not calm her aching heart.

Chapter Four
Hope

Hope watched the students filing in by class and enjoyed the look of their red shirts, white shirts, and grey skirts or pants.

"Good morning, Dr. Fleming," a familiar voice called. She turned to see third-grader Artie Omark in a well-fitting, red wool blazer, white shirt, and red-patterned necktie.

"Well, good morning to you, Mr. Omark." She smiled back. "Aren't you looking wonderful in that smart blazer."

"He's doing announcements today," classmate Francine Harwell explained. "He always dresses up for announcements." She giggled and smoothed her grey skirt.

"I always dress up for announcements," Artie echoed, as the line swept him along.

Leave it to Artie and his mother to really work with the new school dress policy, Hope thought. It was made for them. Too bad not all parents agreed with it. She looked toward Mrs. Egan, sitting on the bench by the office door, waiting to see her. She will have her own peculiar objection to the policy, Hope surmised.

The second bell rang, sending Hope toward her office.

"I'll be with you in a moment, Mrs. Egan," she said.

Secretary Corinne Tompkins smiled and held up a discreet sign as she passed the desk.

An unhappy Mr. Taylor is waiting in your office.

"Good morning, Mr. Taylor," Hope said, stepping into her office. "Sit down." She offered her hand.

"No thanks, I prefer to stand, Hope." He shook her hand limply and did not return the smile.

"How may I help you this morning?" Hope asked, left with no choice but to remain standing though she wanted to sit.

"It's about this new dress code," he grumbled, two fingers loosening his collar.

Hope, locking eyes with him, asked, "What about the new dress code, Chuck?"

He shifted his feet and shrugged a shoulder. "It's a big nuisance; it's time consuming; managing it is stealing instructional time." He sighed and looked away.

"Are you talking about the school dress policy for students or the policy for teachers?" she asked. "Because I must say you look professional and authoritarian in your shirt and tie."

Mr. Taylor's face reddened slightly. He shook his head. "No. I mean—both. Both policies are a big inconvenience."

"Do we have to do this, Hope? Does Dr. Thorstenson, as superintendent, really have the legal right to dictate dress to us?" Chuck asked in a thin voice.

"You do and he has," Hope said. "That is if the code is applicable to everyone equally and without discrimination based on gender, race, or ethnicity." [1]

"But this is a public school, Hope." He lifted his palms.

"That's right, Chuck." She took a deep breath without breaking eye contact. "That is why the parents had to be surveyed first. And seventy-nine percent of the respondents voted for a school dress policy."

"But what about the other twenty-one percent?" Chuck asked, sounding more and more adolescent.

Hope thought of Mrs. Egan waiting, and a knot of anxiety rose in her stomach.

"What if they can't afford uniforms?" He muttered.

"Chuck, I'm surprised that you are bringing up these objections at this late date. You had many opportunities to voice them this summer." She reached for a bottle of water on her desk and drank from it, offering a fresh bottle to him. He took it and drank.

"Dr. Thorstenson held district meetings with every grade level to get teacher input." She continued. "Teachers and parents and students were invited to a public forum where anyone who wanted it was given the floor and the microphone. That meeting went on for three-and-one-half hours. Chuck," she waved one palm, "I saw you there. Why didn't you have your say then?"

He leveled his eyes at her without speaking.

"Dr. Thorstenson ran an email hotline and a blog where every posting stayed there for anyone to read or add comment. He also opened his office for individual appointments." Hope stopped for breath.

"I just did not know how disruptive it was going to be," Chuck said, dropping his chin.

In the end, Hope scheduled a meeting with Chuck and Superintendent Thorstenson to discuss the matter but cautioned him that he was expected to comply, as were his students, with the school dress policy.

As it turned out, Mrs. Egan shared Chuck's issue. But Hope sensed early in their meeting that she was not opposed to the policy. She just wanted to express concern for parents who could not afford to purchase school "uniforms."

Once Hope explained that a school dress policy was more flexible than a school-uniform requirement in that it required students to wear specified colors rather than regulation uniforms, Mrs. Egan felt better. The fact that those colors could be purchased in different price and quality ranges; and all the local shops—even discount stores—stocked an assortment, further eased her mind.

"I'm actually in favor of the new dress code, Dr. Fleming," Mrs. Egan said. "When I was growing up, we had school clothes, nicer clothes just for school. And we knew when we wore those clothes, it was time to learn and get our work done. We changed into playclothes after school."

She had left the office seemingly pacified and with the principal pleasantly surprised.

Hope felt drained at the end of the day. Much of her time had been spent on issues having little to do with instruction, one of the most vital aspects of her work.

On the drive home she was still anxious from the school day and feared that she was to have an even more stressful evening facing Theo for dinner.

What should be my attitude toward him, she asked herself. Indifference? After all, he did go completely cold and remote after I told him I had a guilty past. He cut off our relationship in one fell swoop. Just like that.

She unconsciously snapped her fingers and coasted into a stop as the traffic light went from yellow to red.

With no word at all, he withheld himself from me, her thoughts continued.

Hope remembered the wonderful times they'd shared, the fine dinners, the laughter and jokes, the concerts. Even meetings with the shelter board of directors were pleasurable with Theo by her side. The warmth that flowed between them was quite beautiful and rare. She had never felt such closeness with another human being before—certainly not with Michael, not ever with Michael.

Why, we were on the verge of a serious romance. Completely content together. Soulmates. How can I give him indifference?

The light turned green, and a driver behind her sounded his horn. "All right all right," she muttered, trouncing the gas pedal and lunging the Volvo forward.

Hope's anger toward that driver coalesced with the anger she felt toward Theo. "It's answers I need!" she shouted to herself as she turned onto Canterbury Road. She swerved into her driveway and slammed on the brakes. "I am entitled to answers, and I'm going to have them."

~ ~ ~

They met at a restaurant they had never patronized together. In fact, it had been open less than a year and was on the other side of the city in an area neither of them had frequented.

Hope walked through the door precisely at six o'clock; the host escorted her to Theo's table. He nodded and stood when she approached.

"Hello, Hope," he said in a soft voice and looked at her with sorrowful eyes.

"Good evening, Theo." Hope's voice was strong and even, bolstered by the anger she had nursed for several hours.

They chatted stiffly about the weather and scanned the menu. They chatted stiffly about the menu. The tension was so palpable that Hope wanted to flee. She looked around for signs of the ladies' room and spotted it behind Theo's back.

"Excuse me, I'm going to…" she was poised to stand.

"Hope," Theo interrupted her. "Please. Please let me explain a few things before we order dinner." He touched her wrist and looked into her face with pleading eyes.

The warmth of his touch and his deep brown eyes washed over her, dissolving her anger. She took his hand.

"Theo," she leaned her face toward his. "How could you do that to me? To us?"

He swallowed and looked across the room, releasing her hand. He nodded away the approaching waiter, who backtracked toward the kitchen. Breathing deeply, he turned to face Hope, his eyes unflinching.

"Are you asking how I could have suddenly written off what we had together? How I could have severed our relationship that way? How I could have done all that without one word to you?"

She was caught off guard by his frankness. "That is indeed the whole of it, Theo." Hope said, unexpectedly fearful of his explanation. She wrung her hands under the table, wishing he would unlock his eyes from hers.

"It's very simple, Hope," Theo lowered his voice and finally looked away.

She waited breathlessly until he turned toward her again.

"I'm a convicted felon, Hope." Theo said, his voice low.

She felt brutally stabbed. "No, Theo, you can't possibly be, not you." She felt tears forming—refusing to flow.

"It's true. It's a bizarre story but a true one." He looked away, coughing into his hand. She waited for his eyes to meet hers again. "It's also true that convicted felons are not allowed to fraternize with other convicted felons."

Hope, aghast, looked around the dining room, wondering who may have overheard.

"But I'm not a convicted felon," she whispered, stunned by the label he applied to her.

"But you said you were an embezzler, Hope." Theo said, infuriating her by not whispering. "Embezzlement is a felony."

"Theo," she chastised, "this is not the place to have a private conversation such as the one we are having." She nodded yes to the approaching waiter. "Let's have our dinner first."

"I'm not afraid; I've paid my debt to society." Theo said smugly. "One day, I will tell you the entire story."

Hope winced. She could not bear this talk of felonies.

Rescued by the waiter, Hope hastily ordered the house special and annoyed the waiter by requesting substitutions for the featured sauce and vegetables, neither of which she cared at all about having. In fact, she was afraid she may not be able to eat even a bit.

Theo, now in control of his emotions, ordered beef tips.

The waiter left. Their eyes met, each seeing in the other, the frustration they both felt from the anticlimactic conversation.

Both were fighting a desire to flee.

Should I have left sleeping dogs lie? Theo asked himself.

How dare he paint me with his convicted-felon brush, Hope thought.

Time stood painfully still. They pretended interest in watching musicians setting up to play on a small corner stage.

Just when each felt they could bear the other no longer, a beautiful string-filled rendition of *The Day You Took My Hand* filled the room, effectively carrying them to a private, faraway place.

Theo stood and took Hope's hand; she followed him onto the dance floor.

He folded her against him and smiled into her eyes. Their hearts joined with an old intensity as they floated to the music. Neither spoke.

Losing herself in the mood of their bodies swaying as one to the music, Hope tried to fend off intrusive questions about Theo's felony.

~ ~ ~

A sleep-deprived Hope sat down with fourth-grade teacher Brad Kushner. Early morning was the only time either could meet to address an "urgent" request from the middle school to send behavior records for former Poore Pond student Tommy Grant.

Brad spoke, "As I said, the fact that teachers over there think he needs an individual behavior plan at all shocks me. He was a good citizen in my class, but I know middle school can trigger acting out in some kids. And Tommy did display false bravado on the playground a few times, remember, Hope?" He sat back and sipped from a coffee mug.

"Yes, I do. But they were minor infractions," Hope replied. "And Tommy was over there for the fifth-grade Magnet Program, so they have had him an entire year." She glanced at her watch.

Both studied the memorandum asking for behavioral records and citing district policy requiring *the transmission of all behavioral records for chronically unruly students.*

"There's a new assistant principal over there," Hope said. I will contact him and explain the situation." The teacher waved and left.

Hope lifted the contents from the inbox outside her door.

"Dr. Fleming, Mr. Sellers needs to see you," Secretary Corinne Tompkins called from her desk.

Hope stepped toward Corinne.

"He asked me to call him when you are available." Corinne lowered her voice, "He says it's personal."

Reading each other's thoughts, Hope and she shared smiles of delight. "Go ahead and call him now, Corinne," Hope said.

Ray came through the door and closed it nervously. Hope studied his face for clues.

"Well, hello, Ray," she said, smiling broadly. "What important matter brings you to my office so early in the day? Please sit down."

Ray took a chair opposite her and spread his lean hands on the table. It took him a moment to begin.

"What kind of—-I mean—-what's appropriate for a bride, you know, the second time she gets married?" He asked, his face reddening. He averted his eyes.

"Ray! Are you saying that you and Heather have set a date?" Hope could not contain her joy.

"November first," he said, sounding as if he did not quite believe it.

"And Heather is wondering what sort of wedding the two of you should have?"

"Yes—well, she said she needed to ask someone about it, someone like Dr. Fleming." He looked at Hope. "Those were her words."

"So you told her you would ask me?" Hope said.

"No, not exactly. I just decided to do it for her." Ray seemed to have collected himself. "Heck, Hope, you know how long I've been trying to get Heather to set a wedding date."

She touched his arm, "I am so happy for you, Ray," she said, her eyes shining. "Please let me know if I can help in any way."

"What should I tell Heather, about the wedding? What would be the right way to handle it?" Ray asked vehemently.

"Small and tasteful, Ray." Hope put on her thoughtful face. "Some of the most elegant weddings I've seen have been small."

"What about a wedding gown?" he asked, surprising Hope no end.

"Certainly she could wear a long, white dress. That old taboo is gone now. Practically anything goes today. Not a wedding-ish gown, but a simple long, ivory dress would be lovely and appropriate." A small knock sounded at the door, and she went to open it. "Excuse me, Ray."

Fourth-grader Shannon Stokes held out two perfect, long-stemmed, red roses. "These are for you, Dr. Fleming," she beamed at her principal. "My mom had twin boys at ten thirty last night."

Hope bent to hug her. "So you are Big Sister again this year, Shannon. That's wonderful. Congratulations to you and your family."

"Thanks. Bye Dr. Fleming." She rushed away. Hope watched her go, taking a moment to savor the joy of the birth of twins. Her heart, already full from Ray's news, overflowed. Her eyes met Corinne's, who had heard about the twins and smiled broadly.

Hope closed the office door and turned toward Ray.

"I guess this is the day for Big Life News," he chuckled.

In the end, Ray left with an invitation to Heather to call Hope or stop to see her about the wedding plans.

It's nearly ten o'clock and I've not made rounds yet, Hope thought. She hurried out the office door toward the primary wing.

Hope stopped to admire an eye-catching wall display on vowels. Vowel letters stood next to brightly colored pictures of objects, the names of which made short-vowel sounds.

Headings were in place for Long Vowels, Diphthongs, and R-Controlled Vowels.[2] Obviously, primary teachers had long-range plans for the display. She knew that it would expand as each skill was taught, and rightly so, Hope thought.

She would remind teachers to incorporate the articles:

a, an   the /thuh/, the /thee/.

Before words beginning with vowels, the latter forms are used.

From her own early education, etched on her brain were:

an apple, a bird;   thee apple, thuh bird.

Obviously these forms are no longer taught. They are not common usage and are rarely used by people on television, including the professionals, she complained to herself.

She knew the skill was part of district curriculum, but little reinforcement was built into the lessons.Teachers had to include it on their own.

Perhaps we will have a little drill and practice at the next faculty meeting, she thought.

Hope stepped into Mr. Master's first-grade class where she found him in full flow, instructing the entire class. She waved an open palm at the teacher, signaling him to carry on with his lesson.

Using colorful charts and an old-fashioned pointer, he was instructing the students in the vowel sound, short i. He pointed to each word in a list, and the class responded in unison: bit – dip – hip – lip – rip – sip – tip – zip.Their eager voices filled the air and cheered the principal. She scanned the room to see if every student was engaged. Hannah Hapwell, was the only child not participating; she sat quietly, resting her head on her desk.

Hope went to Hannah and, laying a gentle hand on her shoulder, asked if she felt well. Hannah raised her head and shook it yes. Noticing the girl's flushed face, she felt her warm forehead.

She sat with her hand on the child's back as a student went to the word chart with the pointer and directed the class in sounding the words. Hannah watched for a moment then laid her head down again.

"Come with me to the clinic, Hannah," Hope whispered. "Nurse Sunfield will take your temperature."

Hannah hesitated then took a sip of water from a tiny paper cup on her desk.

"Hannah wanted to drink a little water and wait a few minutes to see if she felt better," Mr. Masters said as he approached them. "She's trying for a perfect-attendance award this year and is afraid of being sent home."

"David, it's your turn to lead the class. Start at the bottom of the list and go to the top," the teacher said, not missing a beat in directing the lesson.

Hope took Hannah's hand, and the child rose. "She'll go to the nurse with me, Mr. Masters, and be checked." She smiled down at the girl, who bravely gave a small return smile. "If she has no temperature, perhaps all she needs is a little rest. Thank you."

Principal and student exited the room as another first-grader began leading the class through short- i words, this time going in random order.

After seeing Hannah to the clinic, Hope resumed her rounds with Trudy Cooper's first-grade class. In the corner, a parent volunteer worked one-on-one with a bright-faced, mop-headed boy and a set of flashcards.

Mrs. Cooper led a group of seven students at a crescent table, pointing to short -i words on a table-top easel. Hope watched as the children sounded each word, raising a red paddle for short- e words, blue for short- i words.

"Class, we have a special visitor," the teacher interrupted.

"Good morning, Dr. Fleming," twenty-one small voices chimed.

"Good morning to you," the principal responded. "Please carry on; I want to see your work." She walked to the bank of learning centers and observed. Each child, after finishing a task, took a marker from that center and mounted it next to his name on a wall chart.

Two boys played a quiet game on a board covered with illustrated short-vowel words. "The board talks to us," a dark boy with beautiful brown eyes smiled up at the principal.

"And we get E-P minutes for finishing a whole game!" his partner, a boy with sandy hair and mischievous eyes added.

"E-P minutes?" Hope asked. "Are those easy-points minutes?"

Both boys chuckled. "No," the first one said. "E-P minutes are extra-privilege minutes."

"So do you get to stay extra minutes in school or have extra homework for your E-P minutes?" Hope asked in a low voice.

The boys laughed softly. "Nooo. We get free-choice time or extra library time. Those things," the sandy-haired one said, suddenly serious.

Hope smiled and stepped on to other centers, appreciating the skill reinforcement and delighting in the students' eager engagement with her.

At a desk near the door, fifth-grader Mark Pryor listened to a first-grade girl read aloud from a controlled-vocabulary reader, both engrossed in the words.

Hope, smiling to herself, headed toward the office. This *laboratory time* was when reading class became most interesting to her. Teachers' creativity was truly evident in their approaches to reading practice, in the morning session as well as in the extended reading class in the afternoon. She made it a point to catch one or the other when scheduling primary-classroom observations.

It was also a perfect opportunity to try new methods from current research—methods teachers had read about and discussed in very practical terms at monthly grade-level curriculum meetings.

~ ~ ~

Hope sat in the lounge, eating a small fruit salad with yogurt and wondering about the status of Mark Fleming's quest for a kidney donor. The last she had heard was that Michael took the test to see if he would be a match for his kid brother.

Thank God it has not come down to George, she thought. Not yet anyway.

To distract herself she began leafing through an old copy of *Bride Magazine* someone had left on the table. The magazine featured several simple, long, white dresses unlike bridal gowns; and she immediately thought of Heather. One dress in particular was Heather's style, classic in design with a contemporary fit— possibly too contemporary in the low, low neckline.

"That decolletage would have to be adjusted a bit," she said aloud to the walls. The magazine bride stood near French doors much like those in Hope's Canterbury Road house. She stared at the page.

I could give a lovely home wedding for Heather and Ray, she thought. It could be small and elegant. And it would save them money.

She headed to the office, her mind swimming with wedding ideas.

A group of fifth-graders, sweaty and over-heated from gym class, formed boys' and girls' lines outside the intermediate-grade lavatory. Several students waved quietly; a few called hello to Dr. Fleming. They seemed more subdued than usual.

Hope gave them a formal smile, which faded the instant their teacher turned toward her.

Both his eyes were black and blue as if he'd been in a fight.

"Mr. Taylor," she said, acutely aware of so many pairs of eyes watching their exchange. "What—-how—-are you all right?"

The teacher pulled sunglasses from his shirt pocket and put them on immediately. "I had a little accident—with a heavy door," he said, false force in his voice. "You know we are still renovating at home." He attempted a thin smile. "I'm fine though. Fine." He dropped his eyes.

She walked on down the corridor, still a bit stunned and consumed by curiosity. Didn't I hear rumors of marital troubles in the Taylor house last year, she asked herself. She could recall nothing specific.

What is the real story? I wonder what he told his students about the injuries. They are obviously concerned for their teacher, she worried. Visions of Chuck's normally good-humored students haunted her. The concern in their eyes betrayed the children's brave smiles.

Chapter Five
Ray

"Let me ask you something, Claire," Ray said to his sister as they had toast and coffee in the kitchen.

"What?" Claire asked, oozing impatience.

"Tell me what you think this means. *It's there inside you.* What do you suppose that means?" Ray furrowed his brow.

"How would I know?" Claire snapped. "Where'd you hear it? In what context?"

"I heard it from a teacher. She has it on her wall, says it's her whole teaching philosophy," he said.

"Which teacher?" Claire asked with doubting eyes.

"What difference does it make? A teacher."

"It makes a huge difference, Ray. Don't be stupid. Which teacher?"

"Mrs. Stonecipher."

"What's her first name? I'm still learning the teachers' first and last names." She drew in breath. "You don't mean that Blue Wanda or whatever her name is, do you? The weird one?"

"Bluewave, yes."

Claire cocked her head and smirked. "Coming from her, it could mean anything."

"No, really. She's serious about it. She's a good teacher, Claire; she makes the kids try really hard."

"*It's there inside you*, hmmm," Claire said, her eyes at the ceiling. "Why don't you just ask her, Brother Dear?"

"I did. I did." Ray chuckled. "She wants me to figure it out on my own."

They brainstormed for a few minutes, Claire making notes on a paper napkin.

After a few minutes, she said, "Well, she is a teacher. And she teaches the little kids." She stretched her words, thinking. "She wants them to become independent learners."

She slapped her brother's thigh. "I hear that expression all the time at your school: *independent learners*."

Ray's face brightened. He took their cups to the sink and rinsed them. "That's it, Claire. You've got it! Mrs. Stonecipher wants the kids to feel they have what it takes to be independent learners." He laughed delightedly.

"It's all up to them." He laughed again and his voice rose. "Truth be told, they're on their own. We're all on our own. That's her nice way of telling them that's the way life is."

"Shhh, Ray, you'll wake Mom," Claire said. She brushed toast crumbs onto a plate and wiped the table.

"I'm not sure that's exactly her point, Ray. But you're close. We are close."

"What time are you tutoring today, Claire?" Ray asked, glancing at the clock.

"I have second graders from ten to ten-thirty and fifth, from ten-thirty to eleven-thirty." Claire said, pride echoing in her voice.

"You're really enjoying the kids, aren't you? I told you how they would grow on you." Ray smiled knowingly.

"I guess I am, Ray," Claire said. "The only problem is that I never know where I'll be working. Sometimes I set up my little math lab in a corner of the classroom, other times in a conference room—that's the best situation."

Ray noticed how his sister's eyes were shining and smiled. He liked the fact that she was enjoying the kids as much as he did. In fact, he got a kick out of having her there a few days a week.

It might not be so bad having her substitute teach, he thought.

"One day, we worked in the front lobby." She shook her head. "That was more distracting for the fifth-graders than for the younger children." She laughed.

"Well, today Hope will probably put you in Mr. Mathews' room. His class has an all-day field trip," Ray said, his voice full of importance.

"That's right, Ray. Dr. Fleming told me that last week. I just forgot."

"Why don't you get there early, Claire?" He pulled his windbreaker off the hook and waved his thermos at her. "We'll have coffee in my office. My break's around nine-forty-five."

"We just had coffee together, Ray." Claire put the butter dish and carton of cream in the refrigerator.

"But this would be different. You could see Poore Pond from my world. Just come early if everything's all right with Ma." He went out the door.

~ ~ ~

Ray waited until twelve-thirty to call Heather at the pharmacy. She never wanted to talk to him while she was working, so he respected her wishes.

"Hi, Ray," she said, seeing his name on the cell phone screen. "I was waiting for your call."

"You were?" His voice sang. "You know I can't make it through the afternoon without hearing your voice."

"We're just a mess, aren't we?"

"It's the best kind of mess," he laughed.

"Dr. Fleming called me, Ray, about our wedding. Did you talk to her?"

"Well, I did ask—"

"You talked to her." She giggled softly. "She offered to have the reception at her house; wasn't that nice of her?"

"At her house? We never talked about that." He tried to picture their wedding reception at Hope's house—in November.

"Mr. Sellers to the office please," blasted from the speaker, interrupting the pleasure of their chat.

"I heard that Ray; I know you have to go. Love you," Heather said, sending his heart soaring.

"Love you, too. See you tonight, Ther-sell." He placed the phone on its base and hurried down the hall, resenting the anxiety intruding on his warm glow.

"Claire is on the phone, Ray," Corinne said softly. Her soothing voice did not keep his heart from sinking.

"Is it Ma, Claire," he said, omitting any sort of hello.

"I'm sorry, Ray," she said in apprehensive voice.

"What's happening with Ma?" Ray steeled himself.

"We're in the ER at County General. She could not stand at all this afternoon," Claire anguished. "I don't understand it; she was fine this morning. I helped her to the bathroom. She came to the table with her walker, just like she's been doing."

~ ~ ~

In the end, Caroline transferred to a convalescence center. Muscles in both legs had atrophied. The doctors told Ray and Claire that the condition could be temporary or permanent. Only time would tell.

Neither of them could bear to be in the house without their mother. Ray had lived with her in their grey bungalow his entire life. She had always been there.

He was not prepared for the terror he felt.

After work, Heather and Jeremy went with Ray to Daisy House to see Caroline. She seemed too exhausted for company.

Heather, herself drained and pale-looking, tried to interest her future mother-in-law in wedding talk; but it fell flat.

Jeremy saw his mother's weariness and the fear behind Ray's eyes and did not know what to make of it all. He complained to his mother that he was tired and needed to go home.

The little party said their good-byes in as normal a fashion as they could muster and left Daisy House.

No one spoke on the way home.

From Heather's driveway, the lighted lamp in the window cast a warm, welcoming glow. Ray walked mother and son up the outside staircase and unlocked the door. He held it open for them but did not come inside.

"Don't you want to stay for awhile, Ray?" Heather asked. "I'll just get Jeremy into bed; then we can talk." She took his hand.

He stepped inside. "I wouldn't be good company, Heather. And you're tired. I'd better go on home."

Heather took in his sad eyes and hugged him. "It's okay, Ray. I know you're worried about your mom. You go on home and get your rest."

He hugged her goodbye, went to Jeremy and hugged him. The boy watched as he went back to Heather and gave her a long hug and a kiss. Over Ray's shoulder, Heather saw her son's frightened face.

They both waved to Ray in his car until the tail lights were out of sight.

Chapter Six
The Bradfords

Helsi turned off the vacuum cleaner and looked around the room. My cleaning at home is getting to be more and more superficial, she complained to herself.

She had always enjoyed making sure every inch of the house was neat and fresh, but now she seldom had enough time for even these quick run-throughs.

Cleaning offices is ruining me, she thought. She had to dust around so many binders, desk pads, computers, and the like so as not to disturb important work, which made her feel she was lowering her high standard.

Floors were the only part of the job she felt she could do properly. She even managed to clean well around all the cords and wires beneath desks. She found that quite satisfying.

I probably should not have agreed to clean Heather's place once a week; I really don't have the time now, she reflected.

She could not get her mind off the excitement of getting contracts from the companies in the building near Heather's apartment. Better ways to divide her time swirled in her head.

Determined not to neglect her family while running a growing business, she went into the kitchen to prepare a meatloaf dinner although it was only one-forty-three in the afternoon.

A single company—her thoughts persisted—leased the entire second floor, so light daily cleaning was included in the lease.

But the owner contracted Helsi's company for weekly heavier cleaning. Tonight was the first night of the weekly service, and she wanted to do an outstanding job.

The downstairs client leased half the space on that floor, and had hired Helsi for light daily cleaning. Those offices closed at four o'clock. So if she could make it there by four-fifteen or four-thirty, she would have a head start on the evening's work.

The second-floor offices were open until five-thirty. Helsi was contracted to start at five-forty-five, but she knew that some employees may work past closing time. This was the case at another client's building, and she found that cleaning around the late-staying workers could be awkward. She would make the best of it.

Rachel burst in the door, dropping her heavy book bag on the floor. Her brothers, Dylan and Robbie, came in noisily behind her.

"Mom, Mom," Robbie called. "Guess who helped with Conflict Managers today." He began digging in his book bag.

Helsi, hands immersed in meatloaf mixture, laughed. "I have no idea, Robbie."

"Someone you know, Mom," he chided.

She tried to think of teachers' names and drew a blank. "Oh, I don't know. Mr. Sellers?" She had seen his photograph all over Heather's apartment just this morning.

"No, but you're close," Robbie said, rummaging in the snack drawer and pulling out a pack of cheese crackers. He went to the refrigerator and took a carton of orange juice. "Mr. Sellers does know this person very well."

Helsi patted the meatloaf into the center of a large baking pan and washed her hands thoroughly. She arranged quartered potatoes on one side of the meatloaf.

"Come on, Mom. Guess," Robbie grew impatient.

"Give me a clue, Robbie" Helsi said, scooping up wedges of cabbage with her hands and placing them on the other side of the meatloaf. She dotted both vegetables with butter slices, sprinkled on a little salt, pepper, and water, and covered them with foil, leaving the meatloaf uncovered.

Dylan and Rachel gave up listening to Robbie's drama and searched the snack drawer.

"It wasn't Heather Baker—Mrs. Baker—was it?" Helsi asked, feigning interest as she placed the pan in the oven.

"It was Mr. Sellers' sister," Dylan piped, unwrapping a sandwich cookie.

"Dylan!" Robbie scolded.

"Claire? Claire Sellers?" Helsi asked with surprise. "I thought she was the new math tutor."

"She is," Rachel said from the living room floor. "But Mrs. Sutton's volunteer was sick today. So Claire Sellers took her place." She turned back to the television.

Helsi looked at Robbie. "How did she do?"

"Great! Great!" Robbie chimed. He thrust a pack of trading cards at his mother excitedly.

Helsi took it and saw that the cards were part of a series of American Safety Forces Heroes, featuring policemen, firemen, life-flight helicopter crews, etc.

"Claire Sellers gave you these?" She handed them back to Robbie.

"May I please see those, Robbie?" Dylan asked from the living room, his face serious.

"She gave every Conflict Manager a pack," Robbie said as he took the cards to his brother.

I wonder if Jeremy Baker will join Conflict Managers, Helsi thought.

The telephone rang and Robbie answered it, allowing his mother to focus her thoughts on work once again.

Ian arrived home at four-ten, just as Helsi was poised to leave. He was bursting with news about a contact he'd made at the coffee shop and some sort of job offer.

She begged off, insisting she had to leave immediately if she were to get all her offices done and promising to hear his good news tonight—every word.

~ ~ ~

Determined to finish both jobs and do them well, she kept a fast pace. Thoughts of home filled her brain as she worked, Ian's dejected face always in the background.

I must be home early enough and alert enough to hear Ian's news, she reminded herself.

Helsi left lights on in each office when she finished cleaning, so she would have a clear idea of not only how many she had cleaned, but also how many were left to do.

Phones rang intermittently in both the lighted and the dark offices.

Who was the call that Robbie took when I was making dinner? Did I hear him say Mercedes? I know he said Snowball. Could the Meadow family have called our house?

The thought of Mercedes dredged up the entire mystery of her mother, Phyllis, and the criminal charges against her. Of Mercedes' frequent, unexplained illnesses and hospital visits. Of Phyllis' accounts of the deaths of her other children, born before Mercedes.

Helsi remembered the way the family quietly vacated the house in the middle of the night. She was chilled by the thought. In her mind's eye, she saw Herb Meadow loading cartons in the car. She had run over to ask him if Mercedes was all right. His voice, his eyes, his entire manner had exuded unbearable sadness as he said, "It's Phyllis who is in trouble. Big trouble."

Gingerly dusting around a large binder and stack of stuffed file folders, Helsi's thoughts came back to the moment.

"I'll be out of your way as soon as I get a file," a tall woman in a smart, black trench jacket and stiletto heels said pleasantly.

Helsi smiled and nodded, stepping aside and picking up a waste can, which she carried to her trolley to empty.

As the woman left the room, Helsi could not help imagining herself working in this office and wearing fashionable clothes like she wore. She certainly did not look like a working mother, she thought, feeling a bit envious.

~ ~ ~

Helsi was exhausted on the drive home and longed to take a hot shower and go straight to bed. She hoped that Ian would not be waiting up to tell her about his encounter at the coffee shop.

But the minute she pulled into the driveway, she knew her hopes were dashed. The downstairs was full of lamplight. She opened the side door and immediately felt Ian's energy filling the room.

"Hi, Babe," he called, coming to meet her with a kiss. "You're really late getting home, aren't you?"

She was too tired to react.

"But it doesn't matter, Helsi. You're here now." He helped her off with her jacket and led her to the living room, guiding her to sit on the sofa.

"Ian," she said brightly. "What is this? Are we celebrating something?" Her eyes took in the glasses of wine, the elaborate finger sandwiches arranged neatly on a plate, garnished with grape tomatoes and balls of fresh mozzarella cheese. She took several nuts from a small bowl and realized as she ate them, how hungry she was.

"That's right; dig in, Hon," he smiled. "Yes. Yes, we are celebrating. We're celebrating a real possibility of a job offer for your husband, the criminal."

She winced at his term for himself but understood at once how much this tiny glimmer of hope meant to him.

"Tell me everything, Ian," she said, sitting back and sipping wine.

"Well, you know how I've been hanging out at Kona Koffee with my books, hon." He popped a sandwich into his mouth and drank from a wineglass.

Helsi could not miss the excitement exuding from his entire body; his face glowed with pleasure. She nodded.

"The last four or five weeks, I've talked with a man—the nicest guy."

"About what?" She asked, her brow furrowing.

"Oh, about everything, everything. But mostly about the medical field, job opportunities—he knows so many types of jobs I've never even heard of in the field."

"Who is he, Ian? How does he know all that?" Helsi asked, sampling a sandwich. She began to relax.

"How does he know?" He stood, spreading his hands palms down. "He's a doctor, a pain specialist."

He sat down next to his wife. "And," with earnest eyes, he continued, "he owns a chain of pain-management clinics—he's worth a fortune; he has twenty-seven clinics all over the state."

"What does this have to do with you, again?"

"We hit it off from the first. In fact, he started out as a physicians's assistant then went on to finish medical school." His eyes locked hers as he declared, "He's a really nice guy; and he wants to help me, thinks I got a bad break." Ian turned away, not wanting to hear a negative response.

"So has he offered you a job at a pain clinic, Ian?" Helsi asked, placing her wineglass on the tray.

"Sort of. He wants to give me an internship." Ian said, not looking at his wife, not wanting to hear her "buts."

"But Ian, an internship is usually an unpaid position," she said in her typical all-business style.

"Don't you think I know that, Helsi?" Ian replied, impatience filling his voice. "Just let me finish. As an intern, I would be training to work in the pain clinic in the future."

"But when would you intern? Your probation will be up at the end of the year—that's only three months from now?" Helsi continued the deliberations.

"So?" Ian asked, frustration creeping into his voice. He stood and began pacing the floor.

"So, hopefully, you'll be reinstated with the fire department. Didn't the chief promise you that?" She pressed on.

"Well, yes; he did. But Joe—that's the doctor's name, Joe Grozier, Dr. Grozier, said I could intern nights or days, whenever I'm available. He'll work around my schedule."

Helsi stopped short of voicing any suspicions of this Dr. Grozier. Who the heck was he? She had an immediate vision of the children left on their own while she cleaned offices and their father was off interning. She suppressed an urge to scream.

Ian, refusing to fall victim to Helsi's discouragement, pushed back. "I could learn so much in three months of full-time interning, Helsi." He looked at her with defiant eyes. "Add to that a year as part-time intern." He inhaled deeply.

"Then next year when I finish my physician's assistant program, I could work the two jobs and draw two paychecks."

For a moment, they stared fixedly at one another, neither speaking.

Ian refilled their wineglasses and held out the tray of sandwiches to Helsi. She took two.

"How do you like these gourmet treats, Hon?" he asked, wanting to lighten the mood. "Let's table this now; we can talk about it later." He sat down next to her, putting his arm around her shoulders.

Why does she always jerk the rug out from under me whenever I have good news, he thought. Why doesn't she see how important this is to me? Can't she see how I'm drowning here, staying home, watching her go off at night to clean offices? Paying the bills?

He swallowed and tried to feign relaxation despite the tension he felt from his wife's body. He flicked on the television.

Helsi's mind raced as well. Why must he complicate an already bad situation, she pondered. He can never see the big picture— the impact on the family routine. How can I take on more and more cleaning jobs if I can't rely on him to be running things at home? I know his manhood is suffering. But won't it suffer more if we lose the house and are unable to feed the kids? First things first. It's not always about him. She could not bear the thought of scaling back her rapidly growing company just when she was hitting her stride as an entrepreneur.

They sat like two zombies, stiffly touching; staring at the eleven-o'clock news, each immersed in private thoughts.

Chapter Seven
Hope

Hope, enjoying a lazy Sunday morning, languished at the breakfast table, sipping a third cup of tea and reliving her time with Theo this weekend.

They'd had a wonderful Friday-night dinner with a little dancing. Their relationship—now back on track—seemed closer than ever. Saturday, they had worked side-by-side most of the day at the shelter, overseeing and tidying. They finished with Theo's barley pea soup in front of a roaring fire.

Despite Hope's insistence that his past did not matter one whit to her, Theo had bared his soul and forced her to listen to an account of the road to crime in his native Biloxi.

Dixie Mafia? She had never heard of it. It reminded her of a made-up name for a group of rebellious teens. In fact, Theo's entire story sounded as if it came from pulp fiction; and he shared more of it than she wanted to hear.

A collection of motels, nightclubs doubling as strip joints, gambling houses, and bingo parlors constituted The Strip, which in those days, was home base for the Dixie Mafia,[3] whose origins dated back to the Whiskey Rebellion in Appalachia, he explained.

Through influence peddling, bribery of public officials, and murder, the group controlled moneymaking operations, both legal and illegal, in and around Biloxi.

"Is this story going to include violence, Theo?" she had asked knowingly.

"Yes, but not in a graphic way, Hope," Theo promised and continued.

When Theo's widowed mother, Rose, died in the late seventies, he inherited the family home and a bit of cash, which he used to open a small antique shop across from an historical hotel on the edge of The Strip. The hotel—which had actually been a grand old Victorian home in its former life—and Theo's shop were the only respectable, let alone fashionable, businesses on The Strip. He called his new enterprise Rose House in honor of his late mother.

Rose House was just beginning to turn a profit when two men from the Dixie Mafia visited Theo and offered him a deal. They would bring in goods to sell on consignment and pay thirty-five percent of all sales. Theo turned down the offer.

The detached way in which Theo began his story had surprised Hope.

Two weeks later, another pair of men arrived just as he was locking up for the night. They repeated the offer, this time blatantly fondling pistols in their pockets and using phrases; such as, "if you know what's good for you" and "the boss wants to do business with you."

Glancing out the window, Theo saw Frannie, a burly, beloved police officer on patrol. The sight of his upstanding friend gave him the courage to reject the offer a second time.

A few days later, a uniformed officer whom he did not know, stopped at Rose House. "How's business?" he asked; and after a bit of friendly banter, he stepped closer to Theo, uncomfortably in his face.

"Gilly cares about the economy in Biloxi. He wants to help small businesses. He wants to help you. Be smart. Take his offer." The officer walked away. When he reached the door, he turned and tipped his hat, "I'll tell Gilly to send one of his operatives to see you, that you're ready to deal."

"I knew who Gilly was," Theo said. "He was a big shot with the Dixie Mafia; murder had become their hallmark. He owned many—if not most—of the seedy businesses on the strip and had been in all the papers. I was petrified." Hope noticed that his voice grew thin in the telling, and he swallowed with difficulty.

"Stop, Theo. Say no more," she said. "I can see where this is going. I prefer not to know the details."

"But I have yet to explain how all this led to my becoming a convicted felon, Hope," Theo said, his intense eyes seeking hers. "That's the whole point of my telling you all this." Exasperated, he thrust his palms at her.

"I know, Theo," she said tenderly. "But I'm not at all sure I want to know this chapter in your past. It's too painful." She stopped short of telling him that she could predict the outcome from what he had already revealed.

"Let's not spoil our reconciliation, Theo," she murmured, laying her hand on his. She looked into his eyes. "Save it for another time, please. I want to savor the joy of this evening."

Now, in the light of day, Hope regretted not allowing Theo to finish his story. He obviously needed to tell her. It would be therapeutic for him, she knew. I'll make it up to him later, she told herself.

What she did not want to hear about—ever—was his incarceration.

A ringing telephone brought Hope back to the moment. She hurried to it, wanting very much to hear Theo's voice on the line.

"Hello, Dr. Fleming," Heather's little-girl voice sang. "Isn't this a beautiful, sunny fall day?"

"Yes, it is, Heather. And how are you this morning?" Hope smiled through the phone.

"Oh, I'm fine, just fine. Ray said you wanted me to call you?" Heather asked.

"Yes, of course, Heather. It's about your wedding. I understand that you are trying to decide what sort of gown to wear," Hope said, anxious to hear the bride-to-be's ideas.

"I really would like to wear a wedding gown, a frothy, wedding-cake kind of gown," she said, sounding much younger than her years.

Disappointed, Hope furrowed her brow. She thought of the simple white gown in *Bride's Magazine*. "Perhaps you will want to—"

"But I know that would not be appropriate for a second wedding, would it?" Heather interrupted.

With great relief, Hope agreed.

"It's just that I didn't get to wear a gown at my first wedding. We weren't even married in a church." Her voice dropped. "I wore a white linen suit; that's probably what I should wear this time."

"Heather, you could certainly wear a long, white—ivory would be better—gown. A simple ivory silk gown would be elegant on your lovely figure."

"You don't mean a droopy, old-fashioned kind of dress, do you, Dr. Fleming?" Heather asked, disappointment in her voice.

"Not at all, Heather," Hope assured her. "The fashion pages are showing many understated, elegant white dresses that are quite suitable for a small wedding. In fact, I saw the very type in a magazine; I felt it was made for you. I'll give it to Ray to bring to you, so you have an idea what I'm talking about."

"Thank you, Dr. Fleming. I'd like to see the picture; I just cannot visualize what sort of dress you mean," Heather said.

"Did Ray agree to having your reception at my house on Canterbury Road?" Hope asked.

"Yes, and that is so kind of you to do that for us," she said, her voice shyly fading.

"Where are you planning to have the ceremony?"

"We don't know; we've been kicking it around. The nice places are so expensive," she said, discomfort in her voice.

In the end, Heather tentatively agreed to both the wedding ceremony and the reception at Hope's house, fretting about all the extra stress on her, "what with the demands of Poore Pond School and all." She would "discuss it with Ray to make sure he would be comfortable imposing on his boss like that."

Heather thanked Hope profusely for her generosity and ended the call, leaving Hope's mind racing with plans for an exquisite celebration.

Hope spent the afternoon designing a handout for tomorrow's faculty meeting. She wanted to emphasize with the teachers, the importance of using proper articles with beginning vowel sounds.

Many of the older teachers spoke that way automatically, but fewer younger teachers did. In fact, their speech patterns indicated that they were never exposed to the rule for pronouncing the article *the* with a long e sound as in *thee* before words beginning with vowels: <u>a</u>, <u>e</u>, <u>i</u>, <u>o</u>, <u>u</u>. She knew that once they realized the value of the skill in terms of better diction for students, they would throw all their creativity into teaching and reinforcing it.

Hope would use quick little drills with the teachers to review the practice. She would keep them light and fun.

Sublime speech was so important to Hope and one of the passions she shared with Theo. "I just do not understand people—educators especially—who are careless about correct speech," she had told herself often and reiterated it to Theo occasionally.

"Teachers and broadcasters are the last role models for proper speech, and we are falling down on the job," she would say to parents who criticized their children's language. "We cannot stop children from ever using the vernacular of the day, but we are doing them a terrible disservice if we do not teach them to appreciate and use formal language. It is the mark of a good education."

Hope thought of son George's reaction to her "crusade" as he called it. "It's too stodgy for me, Mother; there are so many more interesting—and worthwhile—things to think about."

The phone rang and Hope, still lost in her world of language, absent-mindedly answered it.

"Hi, Hope; it's Theo."

He immediately had her attention.

"The natives are restless again, Hope," he teased.

"What do you mean by natives, Theo? The shelter residents or the neighbors?" Hope wanted it to be the former. We have leverage over them, she thought. If they don't behave, they know we can evict them.

"I'm afraid it's the neighbors," Theo said disdainfully. "The shelter website is flooded with emails."

"I thought we had pacified them with the town-hall meeting in the summer; we took the steps we promised. They've been quiet since then." Stifling a cough, she went to get a glass of water.

"Excuse me, Theo, my throat is so dry. As I was saying, one of them, Josh Funke, who lives in the high-rise with the courtyard, is a volunteer, remember? He monitors the bus stop on Saturday mornings."

"Well, they're obviously still festering. You, George, and I will have to meet and come up with a game plan. Would later today work for you, Hope? I will bring a light supper for us."

"If we can finish before nine," she said.

~ ~ ~

After much fruitless discussion and visits to websites of area churches, schools, and halls, George, Hope, and Theo began to think that canceling the Saturday morning open breakfasts altogether would be their only option.

"Churches are holding their own breakfasts, not to mention lunches and dinners," Theo said. "Schools either do not have full kitchens or fees are too high if they do. Add to that the costs for a security guard, and it's just not feasible."

Hope looked through her notes. "That is the case with halls, too: high rental fees, pricey security guards, plus strict departure times." She shook her head and shrugged her shoulders. "I understand that they have afternoon functions, showers and children's parties, and the like, and must protect set-up time for those renters."

"The breakfasts made sense when they were held at the shelter with no additional costs," Hope said.

"But there are no funds in the budget for renting outside space if there were such space available," Theo added. "We just have to stop offering the Saturday morning open breakfasts."

"Let's hold off for awhile, folks," George announced. "I have another idea." He flashed a boyish smile. "Let me check it out before we give up on this much-needed service. Don't cancel next Saturday's breakfast yet." He stood.

"I know we have to pacify the neighbors, but we don't want to lose sight of what we're really about, which includes the needs of our shelter residents and other hungry folks who count on those breakfasts every Saturday. Give me a week to research." He opened the door. "The neighbors can live through one more Saturday putting up with the dregs of our society littering their nicey-nice neighborhood, reminding them that the less fortunate are still out there. Not everyone enjoys loft-style living and a full pantry." He walked away, waving.

~ ~ ~

Hope, preparing for bed, thought of Theo and how warm and wonderful he'd been for the hour or so they had together after George left. Things were definitely better between them now that she knew the full story of his involvement with the Dixie Mafia. He was right to insist on telling me, she thought.

It was painful to hear Theo tell how he finally agreed to do business with Gilly, not only because of his cowardice but also the horror of being murdered. He felt he had no choice.

Of course the goods Gilly consigned to him were high-end, expensive antiques that sold quickly. Theo's thirty-five percent commission grew rapidly. The only problem was that the items were either extorted from people or stolen by members of the Dixie Mafia.

Theo knew it was just a matter of time before law enforcement would come for him, and it would inevitably be at the federal level. The FBI had been working to break the Dixie Mafia for years; they were slow and careful and timed their aggressive acts with precision.

I still regret giggling when Theo admitted that in a weak moment, the antique lover in him had purchased one of Gilly's items that he found too perfect to resist: a stained-glass, rose window, arched so it would just fit in the transom over the shop's entrance door, Hope told herself.

"I knew deep down that I hadn't a chance in the world of keeping the shop," he explained. "But if by some miracle I did, the rose window would be a wonderful tribute to Mother."

Hope found his confession heart wrenching.

The phone rang sharply, interrupting her recall of the delicious evening.

It was George. "You might want to call Dad," he said.

Before she could give her usual sarcastic retort, he went on, "Dad and Uncle Mark are scheduled for surgery tomorrow at ten."

Hope sat down heavily on the bed, tried to picture Michael in a hospital gown, sitting still, remaining calm before surgery.

"Is Mark well enough for surgery, George?" she asked, seeing the thin, pale figure at her door at four-thirty in the morning.

"Apparently so," George said. "The surgeon, Dr. Goldman, is an expert in his field. He will do both surgeries. He'll harvest the kidney from Dad," his voice broke ever so slightly.

"Oh, George, sweetheart," Hope said, her own voice choking.

"Then he'll go straight to Uncle Mark and replace his necrotized kidney with Dad's," he finished with even voice, full of bravado.

Chapter Eight
Ray

Jeremy waited outside the principal's office. Not wanting Ray Sellers to see him there, he hunched himself into as small a figure as he could manage. Each time he glanced at the wall clock, it seemed as if the hands had barely moved. The digital watch Ray gave him was no help; the numerals took forever to change.

Finally, the door opened and Dr. Fleming called him inside. He handed her a note from his teacher, Mr. Taylor. She read the note carefully then sat down next to the boy.

"Jeremy," she said softly, her eyes seeking his. "This note surprises me: you, refusing to do your work? Snapping at your friends in class? Talking back to the teacher?"

Jeremy kept his head down. Hope could see the tension in his small body.

"Please help me understand this, Jeremy." She gently lifted his chin, and his eyes met hers. "What is going on? Don't you feel well?"

He grabbed his stomach dramatically. "I'm sick," he said, grimacing.

"Let's go see the nurse then, Jeremy." She stood and with open hand, invited him to join her.

He rose slowly as if in great pain.

"Nurse Sunfield will check you. Then we will discuss your difficulties in class and call your mother."

Jeremy hesitated, a stricken look on his face. "Maybe I feel a little better now," he said and put a hand to his forehead. "My headache's almost gone."

Abruptly he sat down again. "We can talk now. Please don't call my mom. She's at work. We can't call her at work."

Ray Sellers passed Hope's open office door, spotted Jeremy, and called, "Hey, Sport!" After a double-take, he stepped backwards and came into the office.

"Excuse me, Dr. Fleming," Ray said, looking at Hope. "Is there anything I need to know about my future stepson?"

"Not at this time, Mr. Sellers," she said in an even voice. "We are just beginning to talk about a few issues before we call Mrs. Baker." *Ray is not yet related to Jeremy,* she reminded herself.

Jeremy's guilty eyes met Ray's. "Okay, Sport, I'll leave so Dr. Fleming can do her job." He patted the boy's knee. "We'll talk later."

In the end, Nurse Sunfield found nothing physically wrong with Jeremy; but she noted the tension in his body and spoke to Hope about his anxiety.

Psychologist Carol Davis held a short session with the boy and learned that he was ridden with fear and worry. He worried about his mother's feeling tired so much of the time. He was afraid she might die before the wedding, and he would have to live with his father.

Jeremy could see how much his mother's new job wore her out; and now with all the wedding plans, she never had enough rest.

Carol Davis felt it was time for some sort of intervention. Hope scheduled a conference with both Mrs. Davis and herself for Jeremy and Mrs. Baker, who asked that her fiancé be allowed to attend. The conference would be held at seven thirty the next morning and would end in time for Mrs. Baker to get to the pharmacy.

Ray glanced at the clock. Where was Rosie? She had agreed to come in half an hour early to relieve him, so he could get to Daisy House early enough to catch Caroline's doctor. She would have compensatory time tomorrow, arriving half an hour later than usual. Ray would stay for that half hour.

Heather still had not called back to say whether or not she would go with him to Daisy House. I know she was upset about Jeremy's incident at school, he thought. And she's probably very tired.

Rosie arrived two minutes late. Ray reminded her to go outside with the buses at dismissal then left immediately.

As he drove, he checked his cell phone and found a text message from Heather saying she'd had a rough day and was too tired to go out again.

Disappointed and worried, he told himself he would stop there after he left Daisy House.

Caroline smiled when she saw him, "Hi, Rayley—Ray," she called, lifting her cheek for his kiss.

"Hi, Dr. Crider," Ray turned toward the tall man standing at the foot of the bed.

"Hello, Ray," Dr. Crider replied.

"How's my mother doing, Doctor?" Ray asked, forcing a smile to mask his concern.

"Well, she won't be running the marathon this weekend," he said, his tone light. "But, Ray," his voice grew serious. "Your mother has fought the good fight—is fighting the good fight." He looked at Caroline.

The doctor's correcting himself: "is fighting" for "has fought," was not lost on Ray. "Has fought" sounded final.

"Where do we go now, Doc?" Ray asked, struggling to keep raging panic out of his voice.

The doctor moved to a chair facing the patient and motioned for Ray to take the one next to it.

"We've been treating your mom with moist heat and whirlpool baths, routine treatments for muscle atrophy, or muscle wasting." [4] He smiled at Caroline. "She's been such a trouper, tolerating all the moving about, pushing herself."

"That's my mom for you," Ray said, beaming at Caroline.

"Because muscle atrophy can be a symptom of a range of conditions, I've called in a neuromuscular specialist." Dr. Crider explained. "Our next step would be resistive exercises to build up the leg muscles."

"Dr. Crider to therapy four. Therapy four, Dr. Crider, blared over the speaker system. The doctor stood.

Ray was instantly on his feet, his eyes seeking the doctor's.

"We need the neuromuscular specialist's diagnosis before we go any further with basic treatment." The doctor said quickly.

He touched Caroline's arm gently and shook Ray's hand then stepped away.

"Doctor," Ray called. "When does Mom see the specialist? Do we take her to his office?"

The doctor stopped and turned toward them. "The specialist is coming to Daisy Hill tomorrow afternoon. I will phone you or Claire after she examines Caroline." He did not wait for replies.

~ ~ ~

Ray pulled into Heather's driveway and rushed upstairs. The door was unlocked, so he walked in.

Jeremy was in the kitchen, making a cup of tea for his mother. Ray rushed through to the living room where he found Heather on the sofa, wearing a thick, fleece robe. Remnants of fast-food chicken dinners lay on the coffee table.

Ray's heart wrenched when he saw her pale face and hollow eyes. He sat next to her and wrapped both arms around her thin shoulders.

"Ray, I'm so glad to see you," she said weakly. "You got my text? How's your mom?"

Jeremy, still wounded by his visit to the principal's office, peered at them from the kitchen and waited for Ray to notice him.

Ray, in the midst of updating Heather on Caroline's condition, heard the kettle whistling and looked toward the kitchen. He unwrapped his arms from his fiancée and stepped into the next room.

He met Jeremy's big eyes and dismal face head on.

"Jeremy," he said, his heart melting at the sight of the boy's forlorn face. He hugged him tightly. "Are you making tea for your mom? That's my Sport." He smiled broadly at him, holding it until Jeremy smiled weakly back.

Jeremy lifted the steaming kettle, and Ray held his breath, wanting to help but put off by the boy's determined face. He watched as his small hands guided the spout to the teacup and successfully filled it with hot water.

"Would you like a cup, Ray?" he asked.

"Yes, I would, Jeremy. I'll pour my own though," he said, anxious to separate him from the hot kettle.

"No, I can pour," he said. "Get a cup from the cupboard." He motioned toward the open cupboard door and passed the kettle to his other hand, unnerving Ray completely.

Ray watched as he successfully filled his mug then placed the kettle on the stove at last. He breathed a sigh of relief.

"Where's yours, Sport?" he asked, inserting a teabag from the open box, adding sugar to both cups, and tossing in lemon wedges the boy had ready.

"I have juice," Jeremy said, taking a half-filled glass in one hand and his mother's teacup in the other.

Ray managed to keep from helping him. "Sit down with us, Sport," he invited.

"I have to finish my football game," he said, heading to his electronic screen in the bedroom.

"What did Caroline's doctor tell you, Ray?" Heather asked.

Ray looked at her and shrugged his shoulders. "Nothing much," he muttered. "He does not know why her leg muscles are wasting,"

"Wasting? Why are you calling it that?" Heather asked.

"Wasting? That's what the doctor called it, Heather," Ray said. "Anyway, he's bringing in a specialist—a neuromuscular doctor, I believe he called it."

Jeremy wandered in and sat down in the big chair.

Heather looked at him with worried eyes. "I hope Caroline gets to come to our wedding, Ray?" She smiled at her son.

Ray put his arm around her shoulders, "Don't worry, Heather. My mom would never miss our wedding, would she, Sport?" He turned to Jeremy.

"Why can't she just go in a wheelchair?" Jeremy suggested. "I could push it for her." He joined them on the sofa, sitting next to Ray. "My friend, Frank Branchello, broke both his legs last year. "I was in charge of pushing his wheelchair—everywhere he had to go at school—every day for four weeks."

"Good idea, Sport," Ray slapped the boy's knee. Laughing, Jeremy rose and headed back to his room, "See you later," he called from the hallway.

Heather filled Ray in on Jeremy's bad behavior in the classroom. "It's so unlike him, Ray. He always follows the rules." She furrowed her brow. "Why, he wants to be a Conflict Manager."

"What do you think his problem is?" Ray asked, moving closer to her.

"I'm not sure," she said, lifting her teacup. "The school psychologist talked to him. She wants to have a meeting with us tomorrow morning at seven-thirty."

"With us? I'm invited?" Ray asked, surprise in his voice.

Heather sat up straight, placing both feet on the floor. "I told Dr. Fleming that you would be coming, Ray, since you're practically his stepfather."

Ray grinned at the sound of the word *stepfather*. "Will Jeremy go to Latchkey?"

"No, he's supposed to be at the meeting, too." Heather drained her teacup and seemed somewhat revived.

Ray stood and began to pace. "I can't believe he refused to do his work; he's a good student." He rubbed his chin and stared into space. "I can't believe any of it. Jeremy is nice to the other kids. And he's respectful of adults."

He joined Heather on the sofa again. "Maybe Mr. Taylor was picking on him. He's had his own problems lately. He might be taking it out on our Jeremy."

For several seconds, neither spoke, each lost in private thoughts.

"Mom, Mom," Jeremy called from the hallway, "you told me to remind you to take your new medication, remember?"

"Okay, Jeremy, thanks," she called back and avoided looking at Ray.

"What's this about new medication?" Ray said, instantly sitting upright.

"Oh, it's not actually medication, Ray," Heather said, her eyes still not meeting his.

"What is it then?" Impatience tinged Ray's voice.

"It's an herbal sort of cocktail, supposed to promote natural healing," her voice diminished noticeably.

"Where'd you get it?" Ray's body shook with small, rhythmic rocks. His eyes were accusing.

"I found it at the natural health store, Ray." She rose and started toward the kitchen. "It's harmless and might actually help."

He followed her. "Let me see the bottle," he said, taking it from her hand. He turned the small, green bottle slowly, reading the entire label.

She drew a glass of water from the faucet and leaned heavily against the counter, waiting patiently.

"This doesn't tell you anything," he snapped, handing the bottle to Heather, who took one of the large, brown capsules and swallowed it with water.

He held his arm out and Heather took it, leaning against him as they walked to the sofa.

"Did you get into that yoga class yet, Heather?" he asked gently, wanting to make up for his shortness with her.

"I'm still on the waiting list, but to be honest with you, Ray, I'm not sure I can fit it in—or if I have the energy to go if I a do get a place." She looked at him with watery eyes.

He put his arms around her and they hugged briefly.

"You should go, Ray," she murmured, moving away from him. "I'm not very good company. And I need to just rest."

On the drive home, Ray turned on the radio, trying to calm the anxiety dogging him from seeing Heather so worn out. He noticed a small boy on the side of the road then spotted two older-looking boys in the field. I wonder if those are Poore Pond kids, he thought and pulled over.

"Hey, guys!" he called, getting out of the van. "Come on over here." The small boy moved close to him.

"You look familiar. You go to Poore Pond School, don't you?" He peered into the boy's face. "Aren't you Andy?"

"Andrew," the boy said softly, with frightened eyes.

"What are you doing out here all alone after dark?"

"I'm with those guys," he said turning his shoulder toward the field where the two older boys stood.

"You boys get over here!" Ray shouted stepping toward them. They half-ran his way.

"What on earth are you doing out here this late?" Ray recognized the taller boy, Tommy Grant, who used to attend Poore Pond. "You know me, don't you? You used to help me in the lunchroom."

The boy smiled slightly, and Ray put out his hand toward him. They shook hands. Tommy looked embarrassed but he managed to introduce Ray to his surly friend.

He quizzed the boys. Both had guilty faces. He could not quite believe their story about looking for a missing Dalmatian that belonged to the firehouse.

After chastising them for bringing a small boy like Andrew out in the night, he insisted upon driving them home.

Andrew's frantic mother and sister, Alana, were looking all over the neighborhood for him. Mrs. Billings treated Ray suspiciously and did not thank him for seeing her son home.

There was no one at Tommy Grant's house, but he did reach his father on his cell phone. Ray spoke briefly to him and agreed to stay with the boy until he arrived home. Mr. Grant explained that Tommy's stepmother had been called away on a family emergency, leaving the boy on his own until he could make it home from fifty miles away. He said he had no knowledge of his son's friend being at their house. "My wife makes those arrangements," he said with finality.

The entire incident left a bad taste in Ray's mouth. In fact the entire evening—no, that entire day—had been a mess.

He arrived home to a sleeping Claire and a note she'd left on the kitchen table:

> Ray,
>
> I stayed with Mom for a couple hours — had a few words with Dr. Crider. I'm not sure he knows what he's doing, are you?
>
> Claire

"Oh great," he muttered after reading the note.

Chapter Nine
The Bradfords

Smiling to himself, Ian climbed into his car. He circled the parking lot and admired the attractive landscaping. This is a nice place, he thought, and realized that working here could help him regain his self-respect.

He pulled onto the highway, leaving River Edge Pain Clinic behind. He liked everything about interning at the pain clinic. Dr. Joe treated him with utmost esteem, introducing him to patients and always asking—not telling—him to do particular things.

He liked wearing the smart white coat with the clinic's logo on the pocket. When he put on that coat, he knew no one would ever guess he was a felon. Stop these devilish thoughts, he told himself. Dr. Joe knows my entire story, so I needn't worry about being found out.

Ian did not like to think about the risk the doctor was taking by having him as an intern. He sat up straight in the seat and grasped the steering wheel vigorously, wanting to hold on to the energy he had from his morning work. He felt famished and hoped his wife would have one of her special lunches waiting.

He'd had to fight a battle of wits with Helsi to do this, but it was worth it; he was gaining so much—practical experience, some of which complemented what he learned in his coursework.

The minute he opened the kitchen door, he knew that all was right with Helsi. The table was set with small plates and deep bowls, which filled him with anticipation of homemade soup.

He breathed a sigh of relief. "Helsi? hon?" he called.

"Hi Ian," she appeared behind him in the laundry-room doorway. They hugged.

"I'm so happy to see that lunch is ready, hon. I could eat the furniture." He washed his hands at the sink.

"Go ahead, sit down." She collected soup bowls from the table and went to the stove. "We have your favorite: potato-ham soup with grilled tomato-cheese sandwiches." She smiled.

He smiled back and rubbed his hands together excitedly.

They sat quietly for a few minutes, enjoying the tasty lunch.

"How did things go at the pain clinic, Ian?" Helsi broke the silence.

"Oh, good. It went great!" he said with a grin. "You would not believe how much I am learning."

"Well, that's the whole point, isn't it?" she said.

"Yes, but it's even better than I expected. Much of what I am learning in class, I can apply at the clinic, especially all the regulations for health and safety procedures." He rose with his bowl.

"I'll refill that for you, Ian," Helsi stood. "You sit." He sat back, stretched his shoulders, and enjoyed being served. Watching her, he noticed the black blazer she wore with her khakis. When she turned toward him, he noticed her smart black pumps.

She's all dressed up and ready to leave early, he thought. Any minute now she's going to tell me she's meeting a new client.

Helsi placed the soup bowl in front of Ian and patted his shoulder before sitting down again. She took a deep breath, exhaled, and nibbled a saltine.

Here it comes, Ian told himself.

"Ian, Honey," she began. "I'm meeting a possible new client this afternoon, and I have a favor to ask of you."

"It's okay, Helsi. I'll make dinner for the kids. I have all afternoon to study for tomorrow night's class. Don't worry. But please help me understand this." His eyes searched hers. "How will you fit in another client? I thought you were full."

She looked at him with sheepish eyes. "Well, that's where the favor comes in." She looked away. "Dinner is already made. But you're right. I am fully booked." She looked into his eyes. "This possible new client is the only one left in that complex near Heather's apartment, that I haven't contracted. I want him."

"Where do I come in, Babe?" Ian did not want to hear her response.

"Well, this client leases two small offices. He's just starting out and can afford cleaning only twice a month." She smiled. "So I thought I could hire you to clean that small space every two weeks."

"But when would I clean? I'm either in class or looking after the kids every week night. Did you say *hire*?"

"I have an idea around that," she said smugly. "But first let's see if I get the job. Then we can talk about logistics."

Ian was happy to postpone the debate.

The phone rang sharply, punctuating the end of discussion.

Ian answered it and chatted briefly, giving a series of "okays" and ending with a "That would be fine, Herb."

He replaced the receiver and explained to Helsi that Herb Meadow wanted to know if he could bring Mercedes over to see Snowball, the cat they had left behind when they moved out of the neighborhood. They would be coming Friday night.

In the end, Helsi landed the client with the small space. Not only that, but she also engaged Mr. Sellers' sister, Claire, to babysit two nights a month while Ian cleaned the two-room office.

Claire was Sean's No-Child-Left-Behind [5] tutor at the middle school and during a conference with Helsi about his progress, she had apologized for the handwritten practice pages she had given him. "She was saving to buy a computer," she had explained.

When Claire commented on how much she enjoyed working with children, Helsi casually asked if she would be interested in babysitting two nights a month, for a fee, of course.

"You may use our computer; the kids will be in bed," she told Claire.

"I'll tell you what," she said to Helsi. "If I get the use of your computer those nights, you get free childcare. How's that?" Helsi, not one to pass up a chance to save money, agreed readily.

Now all that's left is to win over Ian, she thought, knowing he would object more to having his wife for an employer than to cleaning those small offices. She had to admit she liked the sound of it: Ian's boss—two nights a month.

Ian required much persuasion to agree to work for his wife. She brought up the subject while they were making out the grocery list.

"With both of us gone at a critical time, things could disintegrate here in a New York minute," he complained. "Dinner and cleanup, the kids' homework, baths and showers. I don't know." He shook his head. "And that's trash night. You know how much trash this family generates."

"Oh, Ian, they'll help. You know that." She looked at the list. "We've already started shopping differently anyway."

"Shopping differently? How so?" Ian asked, eyes scanning the list.

"Well, we've kind of fallen into buying more frozen foods, vegetables and beef patties, chicken pieces. Things that are quick to prepare," she said, adding frozen corn to the list on the table.

"I thought you hated prepared foods, Helsi. You always said they were full of additives." He implored her to admit that.

"We buy plain frozen vegetables, not prepared entrees, Ian. If you read the ingredients on the package, you will see there are no additives—well maybe a few."

After checking packages of frozen vegetables in their freezer, Ian finally relented.

"You won't regret this, Ian," she said, smiling with joy.

"Don't you think it says a lot for me, Helsi, that I— medical intern and future physician's assistant—am willing to scrub grimy offices for my wife?" They laughed loudly.

Herb and Meredith arrived just after four o'clock on Friday, minutes after Helsi returned from cleaning the Baker place. She had a large pan of cheese-covered haddock in the automatic oven and sweet-potato sticks ready to bake, so she invited them to stay for dinner, half hoping they might refuse.

Herb managed a smile and looked at her with tired eyes. "That's very kind of you, Helsi. Meredith and I would very much like to stay." He looked at his daughter's beaming face.

Ian came in from his desk and offered Herb hot coffee. He poured a glass of juice for Meredith. The two men sat down at the table. Helsi invited the girl to have her juice at the table and sat down herself. Ian poured coffee for his wife.

"Robbie and Dylan have lacrosse practice," she explained, smiling at Meredith. "But Rachel is home. She's out looking for your Snowball."

Suddenly, the door flew open and Rachel rushed in, allowing the cat to leap out of her arms and onto Meredith's lap. Her jacket was unbuttoned and her cheeks were red from the cold; but Rachel, full of joy, ran to her friend.

Snowball thrilled Meredith by licking her face and snuggling into her lap. Helsi was moved by the joy Snowball expressed with his behavior and that shown on Meredith's face.

"Do you want to play in my room?" Rachel asked; Meredith, cat on her shoulder, followed her upstairs.

"Herb, it's good of you to bring your daughter to visit Snowball," Ian said. "Anybody could see what they mean to each other."

"That cat is all she talks about now—ever since her mother's been away," Herb said, a slight smile beneath his sad eyes.

He turned toward Helsi. "Thank you for taking care of Snowball all this time, Helsi. I am still hoping—although no one knows how long Phyllis will be in treatment—we will move back to the neighborhood one day."

"What exactly is her diagnosis, Herb?" Ian asked gently, looking away to await Herb's response, as if to lessen his discomfort.

Herb cleared his throat and drew his hand down his face. "Phyllis—my brilliant Phyllis—has difficulty with conceptual thought, they tell me."

"What does that mean in plain English, Herb?" Helsi asked, mixing slaw dressing with shredded cabbage and carrots.

Herb rose and moved to the sink near where Helsi stood at the counter. He put his right hand in his pocket and rubbed his chest with his left hand.

Helsi knew her questions made him uncomfortable, but she had to know. She wanted so badly to understand how a seemingly loving mother could deliberately harm her own child.

Finally, Herb began, his voice low and dwindling, "Phyllis has the ability to hold two diametrically opposed concepts in her mind at the same time." His eyes met Helsi's with surprising candor. "The doctors call it *perverse thought process*." [6] His eyes sought hers as she looked away.

Such as: I am so excellent a mother that my imaginary babies tend to die before the end of their first year, Helsi thought. She quickly busied herself with setting the table, so Herb would not see the guilt she felt from having such uncharitable feelings.

Herb walked to the window and stared across the street.

Ian offered to help while Helsi put finishing touches on the meal. The room was quiet, each lost in private thoughts. But what is it with Phyllis, he puzzled as he laid the plates. And why hasn't Herb mentioned those other babies? They lost—was it two or three—children before Meredith was born? What did she say?

Helsi reminded Ian not to set a place for Lucy since she was studying at Kate's house and having dinner there. "But leave two plates out for Robbie and Dylan. We'll fill them and leave them in the warming oven."

What strange need does having a sick child fill for a mother? Helsi considered, setting slices of wheat bread on a plate and carrying it and the butter dish to the table. She filled tall glasses with ice and water, unable to stop the rush of ominous thoughts. Phyllis had already lost several children. Why weren't the doctors onto her? This was criminal behavior, for heaven's sake.

Ian called upstairs for Rachel and Meredith, reminding them to wash their hands with soap. He invited Herb to use the kitchen sink to wash his hands.

The five of them gathered at the table. Snowball entered and jockeyed for a position at the girls' feet. They giggled and spoke to him, lessening the palpable tension filling the room.

The adults focused their conversation on the girls and were soothed by their laughter and joy in being together again.

There was no more talk of Phyllis' disorder in front of the children. In any case, not one of the adults could bear the horror of another word on the matter.

Small talk about the government and rising costs prevailed through the dessert course of banana pudding, which Lucy had prepared for the family the night before.

Rachel and Meredith exchanged reluctant good-byes. Their eyes looked pleadingly at Helsi and Ian when Herb asked if he might bring Phyllis by were she to get a weekend pass.

Of course, they assured him; they would welcome his wife. They said their goodnights.

"Are you as exhausted as I am, hon?" Ian asked after a few silent minutes.

"Completely," she said. "Why did we give away our Friday night down time?"

Because the Meadow family is in distress, Ian told himself. From the look in Helsi's eyes, he knew she understood that, too.

We must be the only friends they have, she thought. When Phyllis comes, how will I be able to hide my scorn for her—well for her deeds that is?

Chapter Ten

Hope

Hope and Ray surveyed the library and broken window, already boarded up by Ray until new glass would be delivered from the district buildings-and-grounds department.

"The laptop was sitting right here on the librarian's desk, Hope," Ray said, sweeping an arm across the top.

"Clearly visible from the window, then," Hope added

"Oh, no doubt about it; it was kids—maybe even Poore Pond kids," Ray replied.

"That young? How so?" Hope asked.

"That young," Ray said. "Remember, I have the baseball that shattered the window." He looked toward the neat bungalows behind the school. "I spoke to a few neighbors, and they all said the same thing. Poore Pond kids had games going all weekend in the schoolyard. It was unseasonably warm and sunny both days. Unlike today," Ray laughed and gestured toward the light covering of snow on the ground.

"And of course our children know that laptop," Hope said, looking off thoughtfully. "Do you think they entered the building to get the laptop after deliberately breaking the window? Or was stealing it a spontaneous act after they accidentally broke the window? Why wouldn't they take their baseball with them?"

Ray shook his head. "Maybe the police will find the guilty party and answer that question for us. I put a copy of the police report on your desk, Hope."

"Are you and Heather all set for Saturday, Ray?" Hope asked, smiling broadly.

"I think so, Hope. It's a good thing we changed the date to December first. Mom wasn't well enough November first to be at a wedding."

They heard phones ringing in the office, and Hope hurried down the hall.

She saw her private line lit and answered immediately. It was a defeated George saying the Saturday breakfasts were now canceled. Michael had refused his request to sponsor them.

I need a half hour to look at this week's agenda, she told herself. The Baker meeting starts at seven-thirty.

She checked the list of today's events. She would sit in on first rehearsals for the Christmas music program. As principal, Hope felt it was important to show interest and support to the students and teachers. But also, one never knew what religious touches Carmen might slip in unexpectedly.

It was just last year that the talented and zealous music teacher arranged between scenes, a nano-second view of a living nativity. Hope caught it at dress rehearsal and was torn between banning it from the evening performance for parents and admiring Carmen's courage and theatrical skill. In the end, she had been too cowardly to keep it in, choosing compliance with the law on separation of church and state.

The monthly faculty meeting would be held after school today. Hope glanced at the neat stacks of agendas, thick with attached handouts, among them, a new drill page on articles *a/an* and *thee/thuh* before words with beginning vowel sounds.

Chuckling to herself, she looked forward to the drills she had planned. Certain teachers were delighted to emphasize with their students, more tools for sublime speech. I just hope the teachers who do not share a love of traditionally correct language don't get themselves in a snit about it, she reflected.

Hope moved down the list, stopping to peruse the agenda for tomorrow's principals' meeting. The topic, *Merit Pay,* jumped out at her, causing a stab of anxiety in her stomach. "Oh no," she said aloud. Every time an educational leader or a politician brings up the subject, they make it sound like a simple fix, she thought. Here we go again.

The intervention meeting for Jeremy stayed on track and ran short. Jeremy handled himself well, and Ray wanted to believe it was because the boy felt safe with Ray next to him. All parties agreed that Jeremy would see the social worker on a regular basis to help him sort out his feelings of fear.

Hope would schedule several get-acquainted sessions with Jeremy and social worker Kevin Burton this week after school on the days Jeremy would be in Latchkey. After that, they would meet once a week unless more time was needed. Ray left the conference feeling hopeful.

He hugged the boy warmly before he returned to class.

"Jeremy will be all right, Ray," Hope said, walking alongside him. "His fears are quite natural. Children have overactive imaginations when it comes to the emotional areas of their lives."

"Kevin Burton seems like a nice guy," Ray said. "Most of the kids who help in the lunchroom have seen him a time or two." He smiled and stopped at the boiler-room door. "They never say smart-alecky things about him."

~ ~ ~

The morning flew by. Classroom rounds took longer than usual because students had a number of questions about the break-in, news of which had spread throughout the neighborhood. Also, excited students taking part in the music program wanted to talk about that.

Hope had just returned to her office when Chuck Taylor's wife appeared with a lunch for her husband, explaining that the cast on his wrist made carrying a cafeteria tray difficult. Hope had not noticed the cast when she stopped in his classroom. All eyes had been on a student who was leading a math exercise on improper fractions. She made a mental note to see him before he left for the day.

After lunch, the building settled into its usual quiet time when students, well-fed and well-socialized from lunch and recess, immersed themselves in project activities; and teachers circulated among them, giving assistance where needed.

Hope began reviewing teachers' monthly pacing charts for language objectives to make sure they were teaching according to the adopted course of study.

"Dr. Fleming," Corinne's voice came over the intercom.

"Yes, Corinne," Hope replied.

"Officers Clayton and Powell are here to see you." Corinne announced in her serene voice.

Hope stood to greet the police officers and shook hands with each before inviting them to sit. They made small talk about the weather and the high-school football team.

"What brings you here today, officers?" Hope asked.

"We have information on your break-in, Dr. Fleming," Officer Clayton announced, shifting in his chair to face her squarely. "We have identified the perpetrators."

"Are they Poore Pond students?" she asked.

"Two of them are fifth-graders here, and one is in sixth grade at the middle school," Officer Powell said.

"Who are they and have you reached the parents?" Hope asked, looking from one officer to the other.

Officer Powell pulled out a small notebook. "Their names are Terrill Hanson and David Browning."

Hope recalled their teachers. "Terrill is in Mr. Jenkins' class and David, Mrs. Edwards' class." She watched him make note of the names.

"They're both good boys," she said to Officer Clayton. "They have good parents, parents with expectations for their behavior. I must say I am surprised."

"There's another surprise in store for you, Dr. Fleming," Officer Clayton said, his face grave.

Hope searched his eyes, waiting.

"The sixth grader has accused your custodian, Mr. Sellers, of molesting him." He looked accusingly at her.

"What's the boy's name?" she asked

"Tom Grant," he said.

"Tommy Grant? He was a Poore Pond student." Hope could see him in third grade, wearing an oversized military jacket and harassing Anthony Tarantino. "Just when did this molestation happen, according to Tommy?"

"Just recently, Dr. Fleming, when Mr. Sellers drove Tommy and a friend home one night," Officer Clayton said, affecting a casual tone inconsistent with the gravity of the subject.

He stood and gazed out the window. "Apparently, your custodian— "

"He's the plant manager." Hope corrected him.

"Apparently, your plant manager found the boys out after dark and insisted on driving them to the Grant house. It just so happened that no parents were home there." The officer spoke deliberately and slowly.

"The Grant boy's friend ran home through the backyards. It seems that your staff member stayed alone with the boy until his father arrived." He looked at Hope with shaded eyes. "That's when it happened."

"That's when it allegedly happened?" Hope said, recalling Ray's telling her about finding little Andrew Billings out along the dark highway with Tommy Grant and Joshua somebody and driving them home. Tommy helped Ray in the lunchroom last year.

"That's just not possible—not by any stretch of the imagination," Hope said, locking eyes with him.

"We'll have to investigate, Dr. Fleming." Officer Clayton said. "Is Mr. Sellers available now?"

"Of course he isn't." Hope's blood began to boil. "You will not interrogate him now. He is entitled to representation when you do interrogate him." She looked away. I'd like to interrogate Tommy Grant and the other boy myself, she thought.

Both men stood. Officer Clayton handed Hope his professional card and a sealed envelope. "Thank you, Dr. Fleming. Please give this envelope to Mr. Sellers and ask him to contact me as soon as possible." He shook her hand perfunctorily.

"Good-bye, Dr. Fleming. Thank you," Officer Powell said, shaking her hand firmly. "We'll be in touch." They left the building.

Hope sat in stunned silence. She did not want to think about the awful charges. Why, Ray is incapable of anything like that. She thought about the upcoming wedding. This will put a big dark cloud over the festivities. If there is a wedding at all.

How will I conduct a faculty meeting with this bombshell sitting on my brain and heart?

I must tell Ray so he can get to work on protecting himself.

Zombie-like, she walked to the boiler room and found Ray at his desk in the small office. She briefly explained what the police told her and gave him the envelope.

"Ray, contact an attorney before you call Officer Clayton, please. These are obviously trumped up charges by frightened boys." Her warm eyes sought his. "Leave now. Take the rest of the day to immediately start laying out your game plan."

She rushed off before she broke down completely. His eyes, full of hurt, followed her down the hallway.

Chuck Taylor came out of the men's room, holding his wrist against his chest. Hope noticed as she approached him, what a thick cast he wore.

"What happened to you, Chuck?" she asked with a smile. "That's quite the industrial-size cast."

"Oh, just a fluke, Hope." He dropped his eyes and started walking alongside her. "You know what a do-it-yourselfer I am. And I'm a clumsy ox at it."

Hope wanted further information but Chuck was clearly not open to giving it. What goes on at home, she wondered.

"Well, you take care of your wrist, Chuck. Let us know if you need any help in the classroom. I'll see you shortly at our meeting." She turned into the office.

In the end, the faculty meeting became bogged down, not by Hope's pushing of *thee* and *thuh* but by the subject of merit pay. Second-grade teacher Katrina Davis confronted Hope by flat-out asking where she stood on the issue. She had obviously seen tomorrow's principals' meeting agenda, which was posted on-line.

"Since you principals will be discussing merit pay at your meeting tomorrow, will you please tell us:

a) Are you in favor of merit pay for teachers?

b) If so, what are the pros?

c) If so, how do you see it working, procedurally?

d) If so, should it apply to principals as well?

"Katrina, this is not the time to debate the topic. You're premature. We will be discussing merit pay at our association meeting next week," fourth-grade teacher Desiree Osmond interjected. She and Chuck Taylor were co-representatives of the teachers' union, or association, as they preferred to call it.

"I know, Desiree," Katrina said, turning to look at her colleague. "I'm just seeking information, trying to understand the whole concept. On the surface, it makes me think that merit pay would end any sort of job security we might have—or think we have." She breathed deeply and coughed. "If it's coming down the pike, we should know what we're dealing with and who's on our side." She looked toward Hope but not at her.

"I understand your concern, Katrina," Hope said, making eye contact with her and holding it for a moment. She stepped closer to Katrina's table.

"Every time a politician or educational leader makes plans to improve the schools, she/he starts with talk of getting rid of marginal teachers. You and I know," her eyes spanned the room, "that merit pay as applied to teachers is highly subjective. It is fraught with pitfalls. How do we quantify our work? Does it all boil down to student-achievement scores?"

There was complete silence as she continued, "We cannot quantify the ability to motivate, to build self-esteem, to inspire overachievement—or for that matter, underachievement, the negative side. How do we quantify a teacher's ability to help children learn to compensate for severely unmet emotional, psychological—even physical needs? " She moved to center front of the room.

"Katrina, and all of you, please know that we principals will not take this issue lightly. We all need to have thorough understanding since it is moving to the forefront yet again."

Wanting to close the meeting on a lighter note, Hope smiled and said, "We have time for a quick drill in *thee* and *thuh., a,* and *an.* We will start with Miss Fox—Agatha—and go clockwise around each table, ending with Sam Jenkins." She gestured with her hands and kept smiling.

"Agatha, we'll do *a* and *an* first. I will give you a word, and you repeat it with the correct article in front of it. Okay, carrot."

"A carrot," Agatha said.

"Now you turn to Melanie and give her a new word, and the game continues." Hope directed.

The group engaged heartily, making it fun by using humorous words like *nerd* and tricky ones like *honor.*

Their slapstick mood reflected a need for release at the end of a long day and an intense meeting.

Hope was able to stop thinking about Tommy Grant's charge against Ray for a few minutes; but when the meeting ended and the last teacher filed out, it smacked her in the face again.

The faces of Terrill Hanson, David Browning, Tommy Grant swirled in her head—and in her heart. What makes young boys take such chances, she asked herself. Why are they drawn to flirting with criminal behavior? They probably all have computers.

At least, the matter was in the hands of the police now. She would not have to adjudicate in any way.

I want to interrogate Tommy myself and get the truth from him. Of course, I cannot; but I would like to very much.

It seems that today's children—she philosophized—are very much aware of the muscle that charges of molestation against teachers and other adults in authority give them. Rightly so if true.

When the charges are true, child victims have been seriously violated and emotionally damaged, Hope's heart shouted. It's despicable behavior.

But in Ray's case, she was certain that Tommy Grant had made up the charges to take the heat off himself for stealing—not just for stealing, but for leading younger boys to aid and abet him. Tommy's charges were blatant fabrication. Or were they?

Chapter Eleven
Ray

Ray sat next to Claire in Melvin Chase's waiting room. He kept his hands tightly clasped to keep them from shaking. Claire sat with slumped shoulders, staring into space.

"What kind of boy is this Tommy Grant, Ray?" she asked in a weak voice.

"Oh, Claire, we've been all through that. Let's not beat a dead horse." Ray said, his voice weary.

"What kind of man is this Melvin Chase?" Ray asked.

"My divorce lawyer said he's handled loads of alleged abuse cases and he's very good at it," she said, lowering her voice at the word *abuse*.

"He'd better be more than good; he'd better be great," Ray spat the words at her.

"Where's that union rep of yours, Ray. I thought he was supposed to be here at nine-thirty." Claire said, leafing through a magazine without looking at the pages.

Ray looked at his watch. "It's only nine-fifteen, Claire. Give the guy a break."

"Melvin Chase better know what he's doing here, Claire. This is no small-potatoes case; it's life and death for me." He looked at her with desperate eyes.

The one time he had met the attorney—to get advice before calling Officer Clayton—he had not seen Melvin as a forceful or imposing presence. Ray wanted a dynamic attorney, someone who could intimidate liars into telling the truth.

Just then, a tall, rangy man in navy blazer over a plaid shirt and skinny jeans, walked into the room. The receptionist left her desk to speak to him.

"Good morning. You must be Mr. Leonard Aaron," she said, her voice smooth, professional.

Ray and Claire rose. "Claire, this is Leonard Aaron, the union rep. Leonard, this is my sister, Claire," Ray said, masking his anxiety well. Greetings and handshakes followed.

"Mr. Chase will see you now, Mr. Sellers, Miss Sellers, Mr. Aaron," the receptionist announced, opening the attorney's door for them.

In the end, neither Ray nor Claire knew what to think about the meeting with the attorney.

"What was all that?" Claire asked as they walked to the car. "Did you hear anything you could sink your teeth into, Ray?"

"Nothing. Nothing from that Melvin Chase," Ray replied. "I just wish I could use the union's attorney; I would have more faith in him. Get in, Claire," he opened the door. "I'm meeting Heather for lunch in thirty minutes." He opened the door for her.

He started the engine before Claire had her door closed. "Jeez, Ray," she said as he sailed into the street.

"So you can't have the union lawyer because he's on sick leave. Isn't there a stand-in lawyer?" she asked, frowning at him.

"The stand-in is a woman, Claire," Ray said.

"And?" she asked, incredulity filling her face.

He shot her a disdainful look but said nothing.

"And? And?" she persisted.

"And I need a strong lawyer. One who can intimidate those law-enforcement types—big time. Officer Clayton and the detective he sent over have already judged me guilty. They treat me like scum." Frustrated, he ran a hand through his hair. "A woman lawyer is no match for the likes of them."

He pulled into the driveway of their house. Claire made no move to go. "Plenty of women attorneys could stand up to those pompous guys," she said.

"Like who?" Ray shifted in his seat, rubbed his elbows.

"Well, one like Hope, for example." Their eyes locked. "I'll bet she could stand up to the nastiest detective you could find," Claire said, climbing out of the car.

She leaned back in and said, "I'll tell Mom you can't come to Daisy Hill today; you're tied up with something." She gave him a tender look. "And, Ray, if I were you, I'd take my chances with the stand-in lawyer. Women have to try harder to compete with men. She might be teeth-gnashing aggravated enough to cut the prosecutor into pieces."

"You could be right, Claire." He gave her a weak smile. "That Melvin guy sure didn't show us anything. And Leonard—Leonard didn't say one word." He waved; she closed the door.

~ ~ ~

Ray looked across at Heather in the small booth. They sat in silence, making a big job of eating tuna melts. Ray kept lifting his eyes, trying to connect with her.

When they finally made eye contact, he saw faint, dark circles under her eyes; and his stomach churned.

"Oh Ray," she whimpered. "This can't be happening to you— to us." She reached over and placed her hand over his tapping fingers.

"I know, Heather. It's all a nightmare—a gut-wrenching nightmare. God only knows how long it may drag on."

"Are you sure your union will pay all the legal fees?"

"Up to two-hundred thousand dollars," he said staring gravely at her. "I just hope that's enough."

"Now I know what Claire meant when she said, 'anybody who works in a school is a sitting duck.' She said that after Dr. Fleming chastised her for working with a student alone in that tiny mop closet. Remember?" Heather said.

"That's Claire for you. She just makes her own headstrong decisions, not thinking about the big picture." He shook his head. "At least, she had the good sense to leave the door open."

They turned their attention back to tuna melts as if eating them required total concentration.

Maybe we should postpone the wedding, Heather thought. I don't see how it could be a joyous occasion with this problem hanging over our heads. But if I suggest postponing, Ray might get a wrong impression. Eyes down, she chewed each bite overly long,

Ray looked at Heather's downcast eyes. Now the wedding's going to be spoiled for her, he told himself. We should postpone it. But what would that say about us? About Heather's faith in me?

"Are you okay, Heather?" he asked.

She lifted her head and caught his eyes briefly as she turned to look out the window.

Ray looked at her beautiful throat as she chewed. He watched her take another bite without turning from the window. Is she having a hard time swallowing? Cold fear gripped him as he remembered reading that as a possible symptom of her condition.

"Heather," he reached for her hand and held it on the table. "Have you been taking your medicine, Honey?"

"Of course, Ray," she said looking his way but avoiding his eyes. She looked at her watch. "We should hurry; I need to get back to work." She stood.

"But Heather, we haven't talked about our wedding. It's in four days."

She sat down again. "I know, Ray. What about it? Everything's done." They locked eyes.

"Do you think we should postpone it again?" he asked.

"Why would we?" she asked.

"You may have second thoughts," Ray dropped his eyes, "now that I have these criminal charges against me."

He swallowed then bravely faced her head on.

Heather, transfixed on his eyes—so full of heartbreak—did not speak for a long moment. She had no doubt of his innocence. Postponing the wedding would scream the opposite, she realized.

"No way, Ray," she said, managing to smile. "We are getting married Saturday before you start to have second thoughts."

She rose again and reached for her coat. He quickly grasped it and helped her into it. "You're stuck with me, Ray," she whispered, hugging him warmly.

~ ~ ~

The very next day, Caroline took a turn for the worse. Dr. Crider refused to release her to attend the wedding on Saturday.

"I knew Mom was not going to be well enough to go, Ray," Claire said. "We were in denial about that." They cleared away the remains of supper and left for Daisy Hill.

"Have you been working too hard again, Rayley?" Caroline asked when he bent to kiss her cheek. "Your eyes look tired."

He and Claire shared a knowing glance. Neither of them wanted to break the news to her about not attending the wedding.

"Crank up my bed, Claire, please," she asked, waving her hand toward the button. "I need to sit up more."

"There, that's better," Caroline said, smoothing the front of her gown and adjusting the bedcovers. She smiled at each of them.

"Dr. Crider won't release me to go to the wedding," she said to Ray. "And to be honest with you, I'm just not up to it anyway." She took a sip from the straw in her water glass and replaced it on the table gently. "But maybe I could be there, sort of, another way."

"Another way?" Claire and Ray said in unison.

Caroline beamed at them as if she had just brought about world peace. "You could videotape the ceremony and bring me the CD—CVD or whatever it's called."

"We could," Claire said. "It's called a DVD."

"And if you were still in your wedding clothes with flowers and all when you brought it, it would be almost like being at the real wedding, wouldn't it?" Caroline asked, disclosing how much thought she had given to the matter.

"It would, Ma, it would," Ray said with genuine enthusiasm. It was just like her to put a positive spin on the whole thing. "That's what we'll do." He laughed. "We'll make a movie for you."

Claire laughed with him and their mother. "And you can watch it as many times as you want," Claire added.

"That's right, Claire honey," Caroline said. She frowned. "Put my bed down again, will you, dear?" She seemed exhausted.

~ ~ ~

Wednesday morning, Ray sat down with Fiona Fitzenrider, interim attorney for the custodians' union. She barked orders at him rapid-fire:

"Sit down, Ray."

"We all have flaws in our character. What is your biggest character flaw?"

"Tell me in three sentences, your version of what happened the night you drove Tommy Grant home."

"Tell me in one sentence why the boy would lie about you."

When he told her his biggest character flaw was in caring too much, she jumped on it. "You care too much? About what? About yourself—you've been a loner all your life? About your mother—I understand she's ill? About your sister—you fight like cats and dogs? About your fiancée—she has a small son you love? About your work—you've taken much time off lately?"

She leaned into his face, her flaming red hair making him feel overheated. "Let's be honest, Ray Sellers. What do you really care too much about?"

She sneered at him. "It's Little Ray you care too much about isn't it?"

"Hold on a minute," he said, leaning back from her. Claire was right, he thought. She is teeth-gnashing aggravated; she's cutting me into little pieces. He felt encouraged and afraid at the same time.

After tearing his every response to shreds, Fiona outlined her version of Ray and his situation.

"It all started the night you found first-grade Andrew out along the highway after dark and Tommy Grant and Josh Wentworth in the field and insisted on driving them all home." She paced up and down in front of his chair and continued.

"Andrew and Tommy knew you from Poore Pond School and trusted you. Josh went along with them but ran home through the backyards as soon as you pulled into the Grant's drive."

Ray listened as if his very life depended upon what she said, which it did. She never seemed to take a breath.

"Fearing he would go out again, you naively agreed to stay with Tommy until his father arrived home in about an hour. Tommy took a soda from the fridge, offered you one, which you declined, and went into his room to play electronic games. You could hear the game sound effects from the living room where you were writing a to-do-before-the-wedding list."

She stopped, eyed him carefully, finally inhaled deeply, and then exhaled. She resumed pacing.

"Mr. Grant arrived home, checked in the bedroom for his son, thanked you; and you went to your car. When you reported the incident to your administrator, Dr. Fleming, she told you that you had taken a big chance, staying alone with the boy in an empty house, that you should have made Josh stay. You thanked her for reminding you how vulnerable you all were and put the incident out of your mind."

"Are you following me, Ray?" she asked. "I'm almost there." She began again.

"Tommy and a group of kids play baseball in the schoolyard, accidentally send their baseball through the library window; and since the entire lower window glass shattered, go in to retrieve the ball then decide to steal the laptop. When the police finger him, he panics, knowing that his father will half kill him. So he takes the focus off his theft and puts it on you with a nasty accusation."

"How am I doing?" she asked, her eyes smiling.

"That's about the size of it," he said.

~ ~ ~

He went back to work, knowing he was in good hands with Fiona. He invited her to his wedding.

"Maybe I will come," she said.

~ ~ ~

In the end, the wedding was held at Daisy Hill in Caroline's room. It had been Heather's idea, and Hope brought floor candelabra, flowers and a string quartet; and it was lovely. Caroline was overwhelmed with joy.

Claire brought champagne, glasses, sparkling grape juice for Jeremy; and all shared a proper toast with the mother of the groom.

Afterward, there was a lovely reception at Hope's house on Canterbury Road. Fiona came, wearing a flaming-red cocktail suit and flirting shamelessly with Theo.

It was just right.

Chapter Twelve
The Bradfords

This would be the best Christmas ever for the Bradford family. Helsi was stretched to the limits, but that would not stop her. She would bake even more cookies and breads than she usually did, and she would have the biggest Christmas tree yet.

There was much to celebrate: Sean's earning the grades to keep his place on the track team, Lucy's maintaining her place in the National Honor Society, Robbie's many school leadership jobs, Dylan's nearly reaching grade level in reading, Rachel's thriving in first grade. They would thank God for all these blessings and more.

They would give thanks for the fact that her cleaning company had more work than it could handle and that she—a complete novice—was being led toward good business decisions.

But most of all, they would pray prayers of gratitude for the end of Ian's parole! They would rejoice and make merry.

Helsi's heart overflowed with happiness as she wrapped another batch of sugar-cookie dough and placed it in the refrigerator to chill.

It was Monday and her early client had canceled because his offices were being painted. So she had only the eight o'clock job to do.

Ian would be home soon from the fire station with news of his reinstatement.

On the stove were a big pan of Swiss steak simmering and a pot of potatoes boiling. We will have a proper family dinner at the Bradford's tonight, she said to herself.

"Hi Hon," Ian popped his head in the back door. "It sure smells good in here. I'm famished." He stomped snow onto the mat.

They hugged then Helsi stepped back, "Well?" she said.

"Well, you are looking at a re-employed paramedic," he said, smiling a little too broadly.

Helsi could see that something was not quite right.

"What's the catch, Ian?"

He dropped his eyes. "The chief gave me second shift. But it's full time."

She stared at him, speechless.

"I'm sorry, Helsi. But you can pay someone else to take my twice-a-month job, can't you?"

She continued to stare at him, thinking, but who will babysit?

"Can't you?" he repeated, straining not to yell.

She willed herself to remain calm. "Probably."

I am not going to let this throw me, she told herself. I'm a business owner. We are going to have a nice dinner and celebrate Ian's reinstatement. It's not his fault. Of course he would get second or third shift right off. He has to earn his way back to days. She smiled bravely at him. And full time. It's a step back up.

They did have a nice dinner. The children seemed to be making an effort not to complain the way they often did at the table. Ian's obvious joy in finally fulfilling court requirements was contagious, and laughter dominated.

Helsi prepared to leave for work, and Sean and Lucy started cleanup.

She was pleased with the calm demeanor she had maintained. She kissed Ian goodbye, saying, "We'll brainstorm later."

As she dusted and swept, she mentally went over and over the situation. Perhaps Claire would still be willing to babysit those two nights a month for the privilege of using the computer. Would she do it once a week? Or more?

But then I'd have to pay her; it would not be fair to tie her up more than once a week without actual pay—if she did agree to the computer-use trade-off an additional two nights a month.

She had already planned to cancel Friday nights at Heather and Ray's apartment. Now that they're married, they can clean together. Ray is a custodian for gosh sakes. He knows how to clean. I doubt if Dr. Fleming will continue to pay for my services now anyway.

But that still leaves two other nights not covered.

~ ~ ~

Although it was after ten, Helsi was not fatigued on the drive home. She was still excited about Ian's getting his job back. And trying so hard to sort out ways to keep her business going without her live-in babysitter was giving her an adrenaline rush.

She realized how much Ian had done to help her and felt guilty that she had shown him so little admiration. She made a mental note to appreciate him more. And no complaining about all the time he spent interning and going to class. It was all for the family, so they would have a more secure future. I cannot wait to get home and hug him, she thought, looking forward to climbing into a warm bed beside him.

Helsi was surprised to find Ian still awake, sitting at the kitchen table with a manual. They embraced warmly. She removed her coat and sat down next to him.

"I can't believe you're still up, Ian," she said. "Are you too excited to sleep—excited about going back to work?"

"That's it," he smiled at her. "It's been so long, Helsi, so long since I've felt like a man."

"I know, Hon," she said her warm eyes washing over him.

"What are you reading?" she asked.

"A regulation manual," he said with pride in his voice. "There are new regulations for the resuscitators, and I have to learn them ASAP."

She poured coffee for both of them, tore a few sheets from Ian's legal pad after asking him politely, and drew a five-day grid with weekdays on the horizontal axis across the top and *Ian, Helsi,* and *Claire* down the side, the vertical axis.

She imagined a schedule for *Helsi's Cleaning Company* --a schedule that was completely independent of Ian. Now that he was back to full-time hours, did she really need to bring in as much money as she had been? Perhaps not.

I need at least $400 per week—$450 if I'm to keep the accounting student who does the company books.

Helsi penciled in Claire's name to barter babysit every Wednesday, as if it had been officially agreed. I'll talk to her tomorrow, she told herself. I wish there were some way to sweeten the pot though, some sort of additional benefit or payment.

Ian yawned and stretched. He glanced at Helsi's grid. "What's that you're designing, Hon?" he asked.

She had wanted to surprise him with a plan that would protect all his time for work, class, internship, and studying. At the same time, she welcomed his interest. She told him of her goal to free his precious time.

"Then why am I on the grid?" he asked, brow furrowed.

"I'll plug in your interning schedule, plus class and study time—just as a reference."

"What about my job?" he asked, emphasizing the word.

She pointed to a tiny 3:00 - 11:00 under his name. "The grid reflects only your non-job time."

"Good girl," he chirped. "So apparently you have childcare covered every Wednesday night with Claire using our computer while babysitting?" He smiled at her. "And you have cleaning jobs four days per week and a fifth every other week—my old job— right?"

They laughed heartily. "It's a start," he said.

In the end, it was Ian who suggested she pay Claire the other nights, hire her for either babysitting or cleaning, or some of each.

And Claire agreed to it—every night but Friday. She refused to work Friday nights since that was date night or girls' night out.

Ian also suggested that they try letting Sean and Lucy take turns babysitting the two Friday nights per month. It was time they became more responsible helping at home.

Helsi said, "Let's pay them." Ian agreed.

As it turned out, Sean did not want to give up his Friday nights even once a month. But the money enticed him. Six dollars per hour for four hours was too good to pass up. So it was decided that Lucy would work the first Friday in the month and Sean, the third, with both reserving the right to switch with notice.

If the company is taking in fifty-to-sixty dollars an hour, I can manage to pay them six. That's half what Claire will earn, she told herself, sadly seeing her profits dwindling.

~ ~ ~

Phyllis Meadow had a Christmas pass. Herb brought his wife and daughter over on Saturday, the day before Christmas Eve. Helsi had invited them for cocktails and snacks from four to six.

She and Ian were nervous before the Meadow family arrived, not knowing what sort of Phyllis to expect. Helsi did not trust herself to be compassionate, given the nature of those crimes. And they were crimes.

"Just treat her like anyone else with a serious illness, hon. That's what she is—a very ill person with a non-contagious disease."

"You're right, Ian," Helsi said and hugged him. "It's really for Herb and Mercedes, this holiday get-together, isn't it?"

"Of course. Would we have extended the invitation if Herb had not asked us?" he said. "Maybe yes, maybe no."

Phyllis looked surprisingly well and rested. She wore a lovely Christmas red sweater woven with silver metallic thread and proudly exclaimed that Mercedes had chosen it for her. Her dark blonde hair, now subtly tinged with gray, was shiny and bouncy; and she wore make-up.

She looks better than I've ever seen her, Helsi thought.

Mercedes seemed thrilled to have her mother back. And Herb was more relaxed and pleasant than he'd been the last visit.

They drank white wine and eggnog and munched small sandwiches, cubes of cheese, and nuts.

"How are you feeling now, Phyllis," Ian asked as they sat comfortably in the living room, their faces softened by abundant candlelight Lucy had placed throughout the room. "Do your treatments have unbearable side effects?"

His straightforward question surprised Helsi; and she squirmed a bit in sympathy for Phyllis, holding her breath until a response came.

Phyllis leaned forward, resting her hand on Herb's knee. "The bulk of my treatment is drug therapy," she said. "And I have so much knowledge in that area that I can oversee my own regimen."

"But you are under supervision of the medical staff of course," Ian replied.

"That's what they like to think," she said, a subtle smirk on her face.

"Group therapy is a large part of your treatment too; isn't it, my dear," Herb said as if trying to help her credibility.

"Of course. Of course," Phyllis said. "But when you've had as much group therapy as I've had, you learn to give them what they want. It becomes a silly game."

"What exactly is your diagnosis, Phyllis?" Helsi heard herself say and was shocked. She looked at Herb almost in apology. His face was impassive.

Phyllis finished chewing a bite of Reuben sandwich. "I have a syndrome," she said mockingly. "A syndrome that causes me to be overly protective of my daughter, to be anxious about her health and well being to the extent that I treat her always as a patient." Her eyes moved from face to face, slowly and deliberately, as if daring them to react.

"But I ask you," she began again. "Wouldn't any mother who has lost three children in their infancy be driven to protect her only living child?"

Ian sought Helsi's eyes and they mirrored each other's astonishment at how out of touch Phyllis truly seemed.

Ian rose. "Herb, let's put out the coffee; so we can get at Helsi's decadent cookies and fudge." The two men went to the kitchen.

After Herb and Ian left the room, Phyllis announced, "I'm to be co-leader of one of the groups, the doctor said. They told me I have the skills to be a good leader, and it would help me heal as well." She sought Helsi's eyes, but Helsi smiled in her direction without making eye contact and rose, walked to the stairway. I cannot bear another word from Phyllis, she thought.

She called from the foot of the stairs for the children to come have dessert.

Robbie and Dylan came down first and went straight to the televison set where Robbie put in the Spongebob DVD he had selected just for the occasion.

"I'll start the movie now, Mom. Okay?" he called to Helsi.

"Fine, Robbie. You children will have your dessert in here." She brought a tray of sweets and four glasses of milk.

Dylan plugged in the Christmas tree lights just as Rachel and Mercedes came down. Rachel went to the tree for a tiny gift-wrapped box which she gave to Mercedes.

Mercedes opened it, finding a silver chain with half a heart hanging from it. She smiled with confused eyes.

"I have the other half, Mercedes," Rachel said, lifting the chain at her neck. "It means we are best-heart girlfriends. Let me put yours on you."

Mercedes beamed and when the chain was fastened, she hugged Rachel wildly.

"May we give our gift now, Daddy?" she asked Herb. "Will you get it from the car please?"

Herb opened the door and a blast of cold air rushed in. He returned with a large game box unwrapped but tied with a wide satin ribbon.

"It's for the whole family," Mercedes explained. But Rachel fended off her brothers and opened it all by herself.

It was a deluxe edition of the new Scrabble with individual boards for each player. "Oh look!" Rachel exclaimed. "Our family loves Scrabble." She pulled out the pieces. "And there's a board for each person! We've never had one like that before."

Helsi smiled, thinking of their ratty game, worn out from all the rounds everyone in the family had played with Dylan, trying to help improve his reading skills. She glanced at Phyllis. Her eyes were vacant.

After the guests had left, Sean and Lucy arrived home and tucked into the party fare. Everyone agreed that the delicious treats would serve as dinner. Throughout the evening, they took turns sweeping back through the kitchen for another cookie or piece of fudge. All were of good cheer.

Later, when the younger children were asleep and the older two in their rooms, Ian told Helsi what Herb had said to him privately.

Sitting next to her on the sofa and keeping his voice low, he began. "Herb is really hurting, hon. I'm afraid he and Mercedes are going to need as much help as we can give them."

"What's changed, Ian?" Helsi asked with earnest eyes.

"The doctors aren't giving him much hope for Phyllis' recovery. They said that *Munchausen by proxy* is a horrific syndrome. 'Treatment is not very effective, in most cases. Some mothers have been in denial even after being videoed.' He had to give his word that she would not be alone with their daughter even for a minute." Ian stopped for breath and leaned forward, resting his hands on his thighs.

"How on earth is he managing that?" Helsi asked.

"He has a home health aide in the room with Mercedes while Phyllis is home—she has only a two-day pass."

"What's to become of her?" she asked.

"Phyllis or Mercedes?" Ian said.

"Phyllis—well both." Helsi stood. "What about criminal charges? What happens with those? Surely, if treatment is effective and Phyllis is cured, she will stand trial for those gruesome charges." She stooped, picking crumbs from the carpet.

Ian stood alongside his wife. "A trial would kill Herb. He knows if she's found mentally capable of standing trial, she will face those charges." Two loud thuds came from upstairs. "As sick as it sounds, he's counting on her not being cured." He walked to the stairway and listened for sounds of mischief.

"Dad, I dropped my barbells," Sean called from the upstairs hall. "It's okay; nothing broke."

"Are you all right, Son?" Ian asked.

"I'm fine," his voice faded.

"He cannot be trusted with those weights," Lucy shouted.

"It's Mercedes we really need to help," Helsi said, her voice tender. "I'm glad she and Rachel are such devoted friends. That's what she needs right now."

"That's another thing, Helsi," Ian said. "You'd better sit down for this one." Helsi, full of dread, sat on the chair nearest her.

Ian sat on its wide arm, turning to look squarely at her face.

"Herb asked if we would consider taking Mercedes into our home, caring for her. He's poised to go to work for a Belgian firm where he could earn much more than he's making now. And he needs to salt away as much cash as he can; Mercedes' future, possible legal fees, who knows what."

"Be sort of adoptive or foster parents for awhile—is that what he's asking?' Helsi felt overwhelmed by the possibility.

I can barely care for my own children now that I have a business. We're just getting back on our feet after a long siege. How could I take in another child? These thoughts raced through her mind.

She looked into Ian's face with guilt-filled eyes.

"Just think about it, hon. Think about it later when things settle down. We can only do what we can do." He touched her cheek.

His words comforted her. But she knew she would not be able to erase Mercedes' innocent face from her mind. It would stay there, tugging at her heart until something changed for the child.

Chapter Thirteen
Hope

Hope sat in her car in the parking lot of Metro Hospital, mentally preparing to face Michael and Mark, who were recovering from kidney surgery. This new caring-and-giving Michael was an enigma to her. But according to Mark, his big brother had always been like that and had sacrificed a great deal for him.

I suppose I must have brought out the worst in him, she thought and was pained by the notion. But he brought out the worst in me, too. Our union was toxic from the beginning.

She gathered the gifts she had brought each of them—good-looking, knee-length, tartan robes and tins of coffee-flavored, hard candies—and lifted herself out of the car, stomach churning.

She went to Michael's room, intending to get the worst over first. Brooke greeted her calmly and led her to the bed where Michael lay perfectly flat, tubes running from various parts of his body.

"Darling, Hope is here to see you," she murmured and motioned for her to step to the other side of the bed.

"Hello, Hope," he managed to say weakly through barely open lips. "Lean over here so I can see you. These idiot doctors won't let me move my head even a quarter-inch."

Hope leaned over and tried to position her face where he could see it. "I'm sure they have good reason," she said. "You've been through an ordeal."

"You're looking pretty good for an old broad," he said, his eyes smiling.

"You're like an old codger in that hospital bed, Michael. I hope you feel better than you look." Her head was tired of leaning. She lifted it and flexed her shoulders.

"I feel as if a damn truck hit me," he said, sounding like the Michael she knew. "But the important thing is how Mark is doing. No one will tell me anything."

"Mark is still in the recovery room, Hope," Brooke said. "I understand that having a diseased kidney replaced by a new one is a much riskier surgery than giving up one healthy kidney." She looked lovingly at Michael. "Not to take away from your contribution, Darling." She took his hand.

"Michael, Brooke has it right. You have done a very noble act for your kid brother," Hope said, willing all emotion out of her voice.

"Go ahead say it, Hope. You didn't think I had it in me, did you?" His voice had gained strength.

"Frankly, I did not," she said.

"Well, I've come a long way since you and I were slashing each other to bits." His choice of words—apt as they were—offended Hope and dredged up distressing memories.

He squeezed Brooke's hand. "You would not believe how the love affair of the century turned into bloody combat almost overnight. Am I right, Hope?" Brooke looked at her sympathetically.

"You are so right, Michael." Her eyes warmed to him. "Thank God we had the good sense to get out when we did."

"It was your good sense, Hope. You ended it." He said to the ceiling. "Your scars have obviously all healed."

He looked lovingly at Brooke. "And now I have Brooke to help mine heal."

"It's George who has the deepest scars," Hope could not stop the blunt remark. Michael's eyes flickered with pain, and she wanted to take back the words.

"George is doing all right," he said, his voice husky with emotion. "I'm trying to give him all the support I never gave him when I should have."

Hope stepped forward and put her hand on his arm. "George is a fine young man, Michael."

She bent down to look into his eyes. "And you can take credit for that," she managed to say, her voice shrilling above the flood of tears welling in her throat. He grasped her hand, speechless with emotion. She returned the grasp briefly then released it.

"I must go," she said to the air. "Please keep me posted on Mark's progress," she called over her shoulder as she headed for the door.

Hope drove home in an emotional fog. Michael had completely disarmed her with his candor. The razor-sharp, coarse words he used to describe their marriage—though apt—had offended her, made her furious.

At the same time, his awareness of his own shortcomings where George was concerned thrilled and comforted her.

She had given him credit for finally doing right by George, and in so doing, had rendered him too emotional to speak. They had experienced a moment of deeply human connection, which laid bare her emotions as well.

This was uncomfortable territory for Hope. It was more convenient to think of Michael as sub-human, the way she'd thought of him all these years.

Tears streamed down her face the entire ride home. She tried to focus her mind on the faculty-meeting agenda she needed in two days. But this long-overdue emotional cleansing would not allow her brain to access any part of its memory. The cleansing would run its course the way a computer installing program updates allows no entry until the installation is complete.

Will my emotions function more naturally after this cleansing? Will there be no trace of the bitterness toward Michael I have nursed all these years, she ruminated.

She entered her Canterbury Road house and went straight upstairs where she lay on the bed and napped like a baby.

~ ~ ~

The teachers, looking rested and happy to see one another, filed into the early morning meeting.They helped themselves to coffee, juice, and bagels.

No one brought urgent questions about the agenda they had received via email. In fact, Hope wondered if they had read it at all and was grateful that they were not raising issues about the Ungraded Primary Pilot Program or Grade-Level Curriculum Meetings, which they had fought all last year to stop offering for parents. She knew they were still in winter-break mode.

She noted their obvious ho-hum approach to examining their handouts on vocabulary development of pre-schoolers and its relationship to school achievement in the early grades and beyond.[7]

But the principal had their attention when she began her list: "*amnesty; entrepreneur; Mrs. Karynaskius—not Mrs. K; first draft—not sloppy copy; hypothesize—not guess; cartography— not map drawing; alphabetical—not ABC—order.*"

Expectant eyes were on Hope as they waited for her next word. She paused a full ninety seconds, making eye contact with each and every person in the meeting, including physical education teacher, Dave Myers, casually standing along the wall, which he always did. This was his way of reminding her that his subject was not an academic one; therefore, requiring his attendance at routine faculty meetings was a waste of time.

"I know you all tease me about my love of pretentious words, as you call them." Hope smiled broadly and the group laughed. "And I must admit I do love them.Words are my thing, along with commas, semi-colons, and the like, of course."

More laughter rose.

She moved to center front of the room. "But there is good reason for exposing our students to the rich vocabulary— replete with synonyms and precise terms—that constitutes the English language."

"What is *replete*?" Boris Mathews called, waving his hand in the air.

"Full of,"Trudy Cooper said, turning toward Boris.

"Sated or satiated," Jeff Masters said, smiling smugly.

A collective groan arose.

Hope had to put a stop to their getting off track. "Annie, your students enjoy using our Word of the Day Program. What do you see as the value in that program?"

Hope was careful not to catch teachers off guard like that, but she knew Annie used the program with her high-achieving students, who craved advanced vocabulary words and were going to acquire them—with or without their teacher.

It was also a fair question for Annie because she had been part of a committee of three who helped implement the Word of the Day Program.

Annie blushed slightly. "There is great value in the Word of the Day Program as in any program that exposes kids to new vocabulary. My fifth-graders throw those words around with delight. Wordplay is very much one of the habits they have."

She looked away from Hope and around the room saying, "It's almost a competition with them, a competitive game." She furrowed her brow. "But not in an arrogant way. They just have fun using a variety of words. And it shows in their writing." She smiled.

"You said it shows in their writing, Annie," Hope said, nodding at her. "That is exactly the point. The handout I gave you," she waved the blue copy in the air, "describes recent, extensive research that supports the correlation between larger vocabularies and school success. Primary students with smaller vocabularies cannot follow much of what goes on in the classroom and fall further behind."

Hope walked to the side of the room. "Annie said her students apply their new vocabulary to their writing. 'Well,' you say. 'Her students are way above average. Of course they would.'"

Hope continued, "But not all her students are intellectually superior; some are just average or high-average overachievers who have been exposed to vivid language and varied experiences."

Eyes began glancing at the clock on the wall.

"Getting back to *amnesty, entrepreneur, draft copy, hypothesis, cartographer, alphabetical order,* and full names of teachers," Hope summarized, "The point is: even our youngest children love learning new words. They love using them. Even low-average students follow their classmates when reinforcement is regular and varied and a large part of classroom activities, and fun."

Her eyes widened, "And we are missing the big picture when we do not give them every opportunity to add to their vocabularies. They can learn those big words more easily than we can; they have fresh, uncluttered minds. It's the adults, mind you, who begin calling teachers and parents with names like Karynaskius, Mrs. K. That's not for the children but for us—for us and our lazy speech habits. The children can learn them. Thank you. Meeting adjourned."

After rounds, a flurry of phone calls came in for the principal. Proud parents inquired about dress requirements for the upcoming performance. One well-spoken parent, who often gave Hope feedback on newsletter articles, rang to say she appreciated the emphasis on proper pronunciation of *thee* and *thuh* for the article, <u>the</u>. Another parent called with a comment about the same topic, saying, "What's all the fuss about thee and thuh? I thought it was a regional thing. Is that all you people have to do up there? You have kids who can't even read."

Hope checked her inbox and found a message to ring Bernard McElson at his law office. The time of call was illegible; so she took it to Corinne, who was handing a packet to one of Miss Marenko's speech students.

"The call came early, Dr. Fleming," Corinne said, smiling and nodding at the student. "You had just started the meeting. Let me see what I scribbled." She looked at the pink paper. "Yes, it was eight-ten although no one could read that but me. I'm sorry."

"Never mind, Corinne. I know that's a busy time in the office." Hope stepped away.

"Oh, Dr. Fleming," Corinne said following her to her desk and closing the door. "Hope, I'm a little concerned about Mr. Taylor. Have you seen him this morning?"

"Do you mean our Chuck Taylor, Corinne?" Hope said. "Why?" Realizing she had not noticed him at the meeting, she reached for the sign-in sheet still on the table.

"He looks pale and thinner than he was before break. He seems distracted and, well—just not himself." Corinne said.

"Does he still have that wrist cast?" Hope asked, spotting his name scrawled on the last line of the meeting sign-in sheet.

"The cast is gone, but that's another thing," Corinne said. "He seemed to be favoring the arm that had the wrist cast, not using it much. And he walked kind of funny."

"Thank you, Corinne, for letting me know. I hope he and Felice are not at some sort of impasse." She looked away.

At the end of the day, Dave Myers stopped to tell Hope that Chuck could barely make it to his car. "I asked him if he felt all right, and he said he was still sore from falling off the bleachers at a basketball game over break."

"Did he look as if he had serious injuries, Dave?" Hope asked.

"He may have: something dislocated or sprained, even broken. All I saw was how much trouble he had walking. He climbed into his car very gingerly, too." Dave explained.

"That's a good word, Dave, *gingerly*," Hope could not resist commenting. "P.E. teachers can develop vocabulary, too."

Dave smiled knowingly.

"We must find a way to help Chuck. Thanks for keeping an eye out and for your input." She stared off as he walked away.

"Corinne," Hope had an idea. "Do you have a reason to call Chuck Taylor at home, remind him of something, for instance?"

Corinne scanned the calendar. "The fifth-grade curriculum meeting is tomorrow morning. I could remind him about it. But then I'd have to call all the other fifth-grade teachers, too."

"I will call Chuck; you call the others, Corinne."

The Taylor telephone rang and rang. Just as Hope decided to hang up, an out-of-breath Felice answered, "Yes?"

"This is Hope Fleming, Felice, from school. How are you?"

"I'm okay. What do you need?" she said flatly.

"Is Chuck home, Felice?"

"Yes—he's home, but he can't come to the phone right now," she said, her words faltering.

"I will hold; I really need to talk to him before tomorrow morning," Hope said firmly.

"I'll have him call you back, H- -," Felice, interrupted by a loud, crashing noise, dropped the receiver.

Hope froze. That loud noise sounded like a wall crashing. Or a ceiling falling.

Should I go over there? Should I ask Dave to go over there? Hope, too tense to think clearly, was dead sure that Chuck needed help.

She tried several times to call their house again but kept getting a busy signal.

In the end after no callback, she looked up the Taylor address and called 911, explaining when pressed, the crash she had heard over the phone. She had not wanted to give her name, but the dispatcher would not take the call seriously without it.

The thought of having to defend her action to an angry Felice crossed her mind. But she would err on the side of helping Chuck even if it meant offending Felice—or both of them.

She gathered her things and walked with Corinne to the parking lot.

I will ring Bernard McElson tomorrow, she told herself.

Hope ate little of her leftover-roast-beef-and-vegetable dinner. Her stomach churned so with concern for Chuck's welfare and with uncertainty about having overstepped by calling the emergency line.

While trying to comfort herself with steaming hot tea, Hope answered the ringing kitchen phone.

"Why would you do that?" a hostile voice asked. "Why would you call 911 when you didn't even know what happened here?"

Hope was silent, trying to understand the caller.

"Felice," at last she placed the voice. "Is Chuck all right?"

Hope asked anxiously.

"He is if you call being unnecessarily in traction *all right*," she said.

"For what?" Hope asked, ignoring her sarcasm.

"Those doctors think he has a hip fracture. They have him in skin traction [8] for now and say he may need surgery," Felice said, her voice full of scorn. "It's just a strained muscle he's hobbled on for days."

Felice did not warm to Hope and gave evasive answers as to how Chuck's injury happened. She said something about his inadvertently locking himself in the guest room and kicking the door down to get out. None of what she said made sense.

I will ring him later, she thought.

But Chuck rang Hope soon after Felice's chilling call.

"Thanks for calling 911 for me, Hope," he said softly. "You may have saved my life."

His comment startled her. "How so?" she asked.

"Felice and I have had problems for years." He paused. "I probably should not tell you this, but my wife has been abusive toward me any number of times."

"You don't mean physically abusive, Chuck?" she asked.

"I mean physically abusive, Hope. I am a victim of spousal abuse," he stated courageously. "I can say no more now, but one day I'll tell you all about it. Right now, I need sick leave. Extended sick leave."

"You shall have it," Hope said and urged him to let her help in any way, "You need a good attorney, too," she added.

Normally, at the end of the day, Hope would review the events at school and assess which goals she had met. But tonight she needed distraction from Chuck's troubling circumstances, so she read for awhile in the living room.

When she felt calm enough for sleep, she rose and went through the house, locking doors and turning off lights. The phone rang shrilly and she answered it.

"Good evening, Hope. It's Bernard. Bernard McElson."

"Yes, Bernard," she said with sinking heart.

"Sorry to ring so late, but you did not return my call; and it was important that you know the latest development with Franklin Baldwin," he said in a tired voice.

Must I hear this now—tonight, she thought, waiting silently for him to continue. Fully aware that she should apologize graciously for not returning his call, she was too emotionally spent to say one word.

"Hope?" he said. "Are you with me?"

"Yes, Bernard, I'm sorry. I've had a harrowing day. Might this wait until tomorrow?"

"No, it may not," he said tersely.

"Franklin is looking quite fit, having recovered thoroughly from his surgery. He's hired a New York attorney and wants a complete audit of Mary Baldwin's estate," Bernard announced.

Hope massaged both temples with her fingers and sighed.

"Will he keep bulldozing forward until he gets his pound of flesh?" Hope retorted. "Can't you do anything to stop him once and for all, Bernard?"

"Like what, Hope? I've exhausted all avenues," he said. "If the deceased left any loopholes—and most do—my hands are tied to prevent these repeated audits."

"Then go through it all again. Go through Mary Baldwin's documents with a fine-tooth comb," she pleaded. "Find something."

"Retirement is looking better than ever," he said, but Hope detected a subtle spark of energy behind his voice.

"I'll stay in touch," she said. "Goodnight, Bernard."

About to climb in bed at last, Hope pretended she was relaxed enough for sleep. Again the phone rang.

"Hello," she said, standing at the bedside table.

"Hi, Mom," George chirped, the sound of his voice cheering his mother greatly. "Mom, I know it's late, but I just had to tell you this now.

"What, Son?" she asked softly.

"Dad's going to sponsor the Saturday open breakfast." George could barely contain himself.

"Sponsor it?" Hope asked.

"Yes, sponsor it. Fund it. He's holding it at PolyFlem. Isn't that the best news you've heard today, Mom?" George laughed.

"You have no idea, George. Thank you."

At PolyFlem? So far away from the shelter? Hope perused the idea. But she was encouraged on two counts: that Michael wanted to make a difference and that George was so pleased.

Chapter Fourteen
Ray

At six o'clock in the morning on a cold January Monday, a small group of troubled souls sat around a table in Hope's office. They wore winter coats against the chill. Because boiler thermostats automatically lowered for the weekend, the building was frosty and would take another hour to get warm.

"Don't worry, Ray. The school board must suspend you while these criminal charges are pending," Attorney Fiona Fitzenrider said to her client. "It's standard procedure."

"And it is suspension with pay," Hope reminded him.

"You need this time to focus on your defense, Ray," Leonard Aaron said. "And heck, you're still a newlywed, Buddy," he added, his voice reeking with inappropriate innuendo.

He searched the eyes of the others for validation, but no one met his gaze.

"I just hope people—people around here—don't take this to mean I'm guilty as charged," Ray said in a thick voice.

"What does it matter, Ray?" Fiona asked. "You know you're innocent. Your wife knows you're innocent. We know you're innocent. Don't worry about the gossips; they love it when they have something like this to chew on. You did them a big favor."

"But it's the kids I care about. They have to be confused." He took a deep breath. "Are we meeting in your downtown office, Fiona?" he asked, miserably.

"Yes, and we should go now, before traffic peaks."

There were handshakes all around.

"Claire rode in with me. I'll just tell her I'm taking the car." Ray gestured toward the hallway.

"Don't bother. Ride with me, Ray," Fiona said without using her lawyerly voice. "We'll need most of the day."

"That dark-haired woman you were talking to when I came in was Claire, wasn't it?" Leonard asked, his voice betraying his interest. "She was at the meeting with that other lawyer, I remember. I'll go tell her for you."

Ray looked at Hope, who rolled her eyes. He agreed reluctantly.

Shrugging, he followed Fiona out the door.

Snow fell softly as they walked to her red sports car. I might have known she'd have wheels like this, Ray said to himself as he eased into the low-on-the-ground vehicle.

Fiona turned the key in the ignition; and rich, symphonic music filled the small car, surprising Ray. He was sure her taste would have been for loud electronic rock. He settled into the cushy leather seat, focusing on the soothing sounds of string instruments.

"What do you know about Josh Wentworth, Ray?" she asked, breaking his moment as she cruised the expressway.

"Josh who?" he asked.

"Josh Wentworth. The one with Tommy Grant that night you picked up the boys. You know, the one who ran home from the Grants' driveway without telling you." She took her eyes off the road to stare at him.

"I've told you, Fiona. I know nothing about him. He did not go to Poore Pond School. I'd never seen him before." He checked the speedometer and saw she was hitting seventy-nine miles per hour—in heavy traffic.

When she turned her eyes back to the road, he sighed with great relief. Feeling chilled to the bone, he looked at the low heat setting. Sixty-two degrees in the cold winter? Ice queen, he thought.

"Then how did you know the strange boy's name?"

"I didn't, Fiona." He was really exasperated now. "You told me his name; don't you remember?" Ray moaned, a sinking feeling coming over him. *I won't have a chance in Hades if my attorney can't even remember the facts,* he complained to himself.

"Of course, I remember, Ray," she laughed. "I'm just checking to see if you're still with me. I need you to stay engaged."

Ray knew she was right. He sat up straighter and blinked his eyes to shake off a desire to escape into sleep.

"Well, Ray, I've done some investigating of young Wentworth. Evidently, he has a history of accusing men of sexually abusing him." She waited for a response.

"But what does that have to do with me?" he said, giving a wave of impatience. "It's Tommy Grant who's accusing me. Wentworth scurried home as fast as he could."

"On two occasions Wentworth made such accusations; once against his soccer coach and the second time against his stepmother's father," Fiona said, waiting until the last moment to slow down before steering her car into the parking garage without missing a beat.

"So you think Wentworth may have given Tommy the idea to do the same?" he asked.

"It's a possibility," she said as they stepped from the car. "On both occasions it just so happened that Wentworth was already in trouble." She walked briskly, and Ray practically ran to keep up.

"In the case of the coach, Wentworth had been humiliated by him—in front of the entire team, mind you—for prohibited aggressive play on the field."

She pressed the elevator button for the eighth floor. "The step-grandfather? He caught the boy filling his pockets with coins from the man's rare-coin collection."

She turned the key in the lock and motioned for Ray to enter first. "So making false accusations was a deliberate strategy the boy used. Twice."

"It could be a coincidence," Ray said, reluctant to get up hope.

The toasty-warm office improved his disposition.

"It's not a coincidence, Ray." They removed their coats, Fiona hanging both on a rack. "I guarantee you it is not a coincidence."

~ ~ ~

It was just before five o'clock when Fiona dropped Ray off at the apartment. He asked her to say hello to Heather and give some encouragement about the way his case was going.

Heather met them at the door. She had changed from work clothes to clean jeans and a smart-looking red sweater. Ray saw that she was still following the advice psychologist Carol Davis had given them at the intervention meeting for Jeremy. Part of the team's recommendations was for Heather to do everything possible not to look and act ill in front of her son since worrying about her had consumed him. Spending all after-work hours in a frumpy robe was not her style, and Jeremy knew it.

Ray kissed his wife and offered Fiona a coffee or coke.

"What smells so good, Heather?" Fiona asked. "Are you cooking?"

"I made a big pot of chili," she said, turning to the stove to stir it. Fiona followed her and inhaled the good aroma.

Ray noticed the table set for four and winced inside.

"Why don't you join us for supper?" Heather smiled at the attorney.

"Oh, I couldn't impose," Fiona said modestly.

"I have cornbread," Heather said, eyebrows raised.

"Take some home, Fiona, if you can't stay," Ray said too quickly, looking at Heather.

Fiona caught the fleeting glance between husband and wife and understood. "May I?" she smiled genuinely. "I'd love to take some home, please."

"I'll pack it, Hon," Ray said.

Heather thanked him and called Jeremy to come say hello to Ms. Fitzenrider. He came from his room in sock feet and greeted her shyly, his face a mask of confusion.

"This is the woman who's helping Ray solve his problem, Jeremy," Heather said, her eyes searching Fiona's for clues.

Fiona bent down and shook his hand. "You have strong hands, Jeremy; you're either a pianist or a video-game whiz?"

He nodded his head and smiled. He raised his eyebrows at his mother who nodded approval for him to leave the room.

"How are things going, Fiona?" Heather asked in a low voice.

"We covered so much ground today, Heather," she said, smiling slyly. "We're going to shoot all kinds of holes in the prosecution's so-called evidence—it's all circumstantial."

~ ~ ~

The little family had a quiet dinner, carefully steering the conversation away from Heather's health and toward Jeremy's day.

Ray asked him if he had started training for the conflict-management squad.

"It starts next week," he said, excitedly. "We get our pinnies and badges at the first meeting." His face glowed.

"Ray, will you teach me to sew? We have to sew the badge on the pinny at home." Jeremy said, furrowing his brow.

"I'll sew it on for you, Sweetheart," Heather said lovingly.

Loud rapping at the door interrupted the snug family.

Jeremy ran from the window to the door and opened it.

"Here's my favorite boy!" Claire said, hugging him.

"Hi Aunt Claire," he said. "Who's that?"

Claire walked in, followed by Leonard Aaron.

"This is Mr. Aaron, Jeremy. He works with Ray." She glanced toward, but not at, her brother. "He came with me to drop off Ray's car."

Heather invited them to sit for a minute and ended up happily offering them chili and cornbread.

They were surprisingly good company, and Ray noticed how well Leonard fit in with the family. He even played video games with Jeremy. I guess he's not a bad guy, he said to himself.

But he couldn't help resenting the way he had moved in on Claire so fast. He did not like her flushed face and giddiness either.

He felt ashamed of himself but nonetheless resentful. But the fact that they were there took his—and Heather's—minds off the horrible charges he faced.

Chapter Fifteen
The Bradfords

"It's really great that your weekend starts on Friday, Ian," Helsi said. Taking a break from studying, he poured himself a glass of iced tea and offered her one.

"No thanks, Ian, I have my juice here. As I was saying," she looked expectantly at him.

"I know, Hon. It is great. But come Sunday afternoon and I have to go to work, it's not so good." He looked over her shoulder at the ledger. "So you're getting the hang of this bookkeeping thing, are you?"

"I believe I am; I rather enjoy it, too." She smiled at him and continued writing figures, Ian watching her closely.

"You took that online course, Helsi. Isn't the idea for you to keep your books online? That's so much writing."

"Yes, that's the idea. But I want to practice on paper first. I can see the whole picture that way." She sipped from her glass. "As soon as I'm confident, I'll transfer to the computer. "But I do like having a paper copy."

"But you can print out those completed pages on the computer and keep them in a binder. Then you'll have paper copies."

"I know. I know. I'll get there. Don't you have to get back to your books?" she asked with irony.

Ian looked at his watch. "What time is Lucy due home? "When do we pick up Sean at the game? It's ten-twenty now?"

"Lucy is sleeping at Marcy's house, remember?" She stretched her shoulders and took deep breaths. "And Kyle's father is bringing Sean home after the game and pizza."

"Let's quit for the night, Helsi," he said softly. "Relax a little."

"You don't have to ask me twice," she said gathering her ledger and papers. "Maybe we can find something decent on the movie channel."

The doorbell rang and Ian answered it. Helsi heard voices then Ian came in carrying an envelope. "Claire dropped off her and Carol's jobcards." He handed the envelope to Helsi.

"You have a good system going now, don't you, Hon? That was clever of you to hire Carol Billings and Claire both for Friday nights. It gives you a little catch-up time, doesn't it?" Ian took the remote.

"Well, yes, but I have to do the books myself now," she reminded him.

"Oh, I forgot to tell you, Helsi." He settled on a channel and sat on the sofa next to her. "Herb called yesterday. He wants to bring Phyllis by this Sunday. I invited them for lunch."

"Mercedes, too, of course?" she asked.

"Yes. That will make Rachel happy, won't it?" he laughed.

"Let's make it a brunch, Ian," she said. "What time did you say?"

"Eleven-thirty, since I leave for work at two-thirty."

"Perfect for brunch," Helsi smiled.

~ ~ ~

Sunday came quickly. The boys begged to be excused from the brunch and ended up getting dropped off at the bowling alley. Lucy agreed to help in the kitchen, and Rachel set up the deluxe Scrabble game in her bedroom.

Spinach-cheese frittata and turkey sausage were in the warming oven. Lucy prepared lovely fresh fruit cups and placed them on the table. From tube biscuits Ian made his favorite cinnamon rolls along with small breakfast pizzas for the children.

Helsi, Ian, and their guests were having coffee after the meal. Lucy worked at the computer upstairs while Rachel entertained Mercedes in her bedroom. Helsi had reminded herself not to ask personal questions this time, and she was determined to stick to it.

It was Phyllis who brought up the matter.

"I'll be moving to a new facility soon," she announced. Ian looked at Herb whose poker face revealed little. But Ian could see the dread in his eyes. He glanced sideways at Helsi, their eyes meeting for only an instant.

"Don't you think you should wait until it's definite, Phyllis, before talking about it?" Herb said wearily.

"It is definite," she said. "They can't wait to get rid of me; they know I know too much." She looked at the others smugly.

"Where will you be going, Phyllis?" Ian asked, as if trying to small-talk a big subject into idle chitchat.

"I am transferring to a less-restrictive hospital," she said, composing herself with another sip of coffee.

"Less restrictive sounds like a good thing," Ian said, looking at Herb.

Herb nodded and began to speak. He cut himself off after two syllables.

"You're darn right it's a good thing," Phyllis said adamantly. "I'll have a little independence, may even get to help out from time to time."

"Help in what way, Phyllis? Not with patients?" Helsi asked, breaking her own rule.

"With patients," Phyllis said, defying her friend. "There will be other women like me—overprotective of their children, overprotective to a fault." She looked at each of them in turn. "I can be a real source of support for those women because I know what they've gone through."

"Phyllis, dear, don't get your hopes up about helping with patients," Herb said.

"Of course I'll be helping, Herb. That's the main reason they're transferring me; they're swamped, and they need an experienced person like me to lend a hand."

The pain her remarks caused Herb was palpable. It filled the room.

Ian checked his watch and looked at Helsi.

"Last round of coffee, anyone?" she asked. Phyllis lifted her cup, and Helsi filled it halfway.

Phyllis added sugar and cream, stirring thoroughly. She took a large drink and smiled at the others.

"Dr. Felton has to be careful, I know. But he's already indicated he's counting on me." Looking down, she began to twist the corner of her linen napkin intensely. "He said that the new hospital will be a better placement for me because of my years of struggle with this—this syndrome. 'You're a living example of the worst form of this condition, Phyllis,' he told me. 'It's the best we can do for you and your family at this time.' "

"Now I ask you," she looked up from the maimed napkin. "Dr. Felton knows how much I've suffered; and he's sending me to the best facility he can find. What does that tell you about his confidence in me?"

She pinched off a piece of cinnamon roll, popped it into her mouth, and took another drink of coffee.

Silent tension took over the room. Herb went to the stairs and called Mercedes.

Ian stood, stretched his shoulders. "It was nice of you to come. Good luck to you, Phyllis."

"Ian leaves for work in twenty minutes," Helsi said to Phyllis, holding out her coat.

Lucy and Rachel came down to say their good-byes. Mercedes hugged Lucy and Rachel then turned just as Phyllis engulfed her daughter in a dramatic hug.

Every pair of adult eyes misted over at the poignancy of this delusional woman desperately hugging the beautiful daughter she was unable to care for on her own.

Helsi and the girls walked them out to the car. Herb hung back for a private moment with Ian. He shook his head forlornly.

"Ian, I must tell you." He lowered his voice reverently. "My Phyllis has been diagnosed with Munchausen by Proxy Syndrome. She's moving from a psychiatric hospital to the State Hospital for the Criminally Insane." His voice broke. "She's been doing things to make Mercedes sick. She could have killed her."

"That's bad, Herb. That's bad." Ian put both hands on the man's shoulders. "Let me know what I can do."

"I already have, Ian," he said, his voice barely discernible.

"Keep us posted, Buddy," Ian said, his heart sinking.

~ ~ ~

It was nearly midnight when Ian came in the door from work. He had planned to wait until morning to tell his wife Herb's news; but there she was, surrounded by a tableful of invoices, job cards, and her prized ledger. Maybe we can talk, he hoped.

"You're still working, Hon? It's late. How about taking a break with me?" Ian asked, squeezing her shoulders when she did not get up to greet him.

"I must finish these entries, Ian, I'm sorry." She spoke without looking up from her work. "Anyway, you need to get to bed."

Finally, she looked at her husband. "Remember, you have to drive Robbie to school on your way to the clinic. He has that huge health project on the circulatory system."

"I thought you were driving him," Ian said, pouring ginger ale over ice. "Would you like one, Helsi?"

"Maybe I will have one, thanks." She stood. "I can't drive Robbie; something's come up." She gathered her papers and put them away.

"What's come up since one-thirty on a Sunday afternoon?" he asked, fighting off annoyance.

"Mary Cartwright called. Her husband's in the hospital with severe gallstones, so she can't make it to the Valentine Breakfast for Honor Society students." Helsi gave great attention to drinking her ginger ale. "I promised to fill in for her at seven," she said meekly.

"Well, you'll just have to work around driving Robbie," Ian said stubbornly. "What time can he be dropped off?"

"No earlier than seven-thirty, Ian. There's no supervision before that."

"Won't work for me," Ian shook his head. "I could never make it all the way to River Edge by eight o'clock. "You'll just have to go later to the middle school; that's all there is to it."

He rinsed his glass and put it in the dishwasher. "Coming to bed?" He went upstairs.

Helsi fought off the feelings of resentment threatening to engulf her. Why is he so snippy, she thought. Sure, he has too much on his plate; but so do I.

He has his internship three mornings a week, his class twice; and he doesn't start work until two in the afternoon, she mentally outlined. There are twelve hours in a day. Every day.

She could not let go. And what do I have? I have a company to manage, backbreaking cleaning two nights a week—late nights, a family to care for, and a house to run.

She thought briefly of what Ian had been through—for making a stupid choice—and the way he had to fight so to protect his study time, then chose to disregard it. Her festering continued.

They lay stiffly alongside each other in bed.

Helsi restlessly kept changing positions. The mental self-torture began again. And he is actually considering taking in Mercedes when Herb goes to work in Belgium this spring. I cannot believe it.

But she knew she could never turn her back on the child.

Because the argument with Helsi usurped his necessary calming time, Ian was still wound up from work. He lay in a fetal position, pretending to sleep.

Why must she always do this, he wondered. We both do it. When things pile up, we go at one another's throats instead of calmly discussing the situation. I guess we're too much alike. We both zoom right to frustration level.

Ian knew they were both overextended, trying to do far too much; but that's just the way it was. Their friends were all on the same rollercoaster.

How can I possibly tell her now that Herb all but said he is counting on us to take in Mercedes? It could push her over the edge.

Chapter Sixteen
Hope

Dr. Fleming sat quietly in the back row of Marla Sutton's class for identified learning-disabled third and fourth graders. She always enjoyed observing this small group on a casual basis when she could really immerse herself in the flow. Ms. Sutton often invited her to participate with students in their activities; discovery or drill.

But today she was here for a formal evaluation, which required her to focus on Marla's performance within specific criteria for sound teaching. She would take careful notes.

Ms. Sutton knew how to use flexible groups to help students strengthen particular skills, and she knew how to make drill and practice more like playing games than drilling and practicing.

The lesson on cause and effect was structured after the popular television game show, *Wheel of Fortune*; and students were highly motivated. The excited engagement of the children in hands-on learning delighted Hope.

"Dr. Fleming, are you there?" From the speaker, came Corinne's voice, habitually serene but with a subtle urgency.

"Yes, Mrs. Tompkins, what is it?" Hope called, made uncomfortable by the disruption of the flow in such a joyful class.

"Dr. Fleming, you are needed at once in the office, please," Corinne stated. The undertone of urgency, barely detectable to most, was not lost on Hope. She apologized to Ms. Sutton and the children and hurried out.

Descending the stairway, she heard the roar of sirens in the distance and felt her heart quicken. She hurried toward the clinic, but Nurse Sunfield caught her at the cafeteria door and led her to a student lying on a blanket on the floor. She explained briefly that a folding table another student was moving had fallen against him.

"Why, Julian Barrett, what's happened to you?" Hope asked, noting bloody gauze squares on his head. She wanted to know how well he could speak and comprehend after a head injury.

"I was setting out the milk crates." He lifted his head; Hope patted it back down. "David tried to move the table——I guess I was in his way," Julian said, swallowing.

"It's okay, Julian," Hope said, encouraged by his alertness and clear speech. She patted his arm, not liking his pale color.

The nurse turned away from the boy and lowered her voice, "David's in the clinic now. He's beside himself with worry about Julian. Corinne called his mother; she's on her way."

"My foot caught in the wheel, I think," he continued, needing to explain. "I didn't mean to. The wheels swivel." Tears filling his eyes, he turned his face away. Hope patted him again.

Ray Sellers' substitute, Joe Maynor, stood helplessly on the sidelines, his face full of unmasked terror.

Two paramedics walked in with equipment and a stretcher. They quickly began examining Julian and asking questions of Joe, the nurse, and the boy, all the while proceeding with calm efficiency.

"Have you reached the parents, Nurse Sunfield?" Hope asked. The nurse let go of Julian's hand and rose.

"I have calls in for both parents, but I reached the grandmother. She is on her way here." the nurse said.

Concern and fear filled the room.

The din of classes preparing to line up for lunch rose from the nearby primary wing. Hope and Joe checked their watches. They looked anxiously at the patient and the paramedics. It was past time to finish setting up for lunch.

"His vitals are stable, but there is indication of injury distress. We're taking him to Lakeside ER," a paramedic said.

"I'll accompany Julian, You will bring me back here," Hope announced. They nodded. She hurried to the office for her purse and phone, planning to call her supervisor en route.

"Corinne, ask Julian's grandmother to meet us at the hospital. And send for Jeff Masters' student teacher to help Joe with first lunch. He's young and strong—and plans to become a principal."

She hurried away, calling over her shoulder, "This will be good clinical experience for him."

~ ~ ~

In the end, Julian had suffered a deep cut with many stitches required. He also had a concussion. Doctors were worried about long-term effects from such a head injury and prescribed the wearing of a protective half-helmet every day for several weeks.

Julian soldiered on like the even-tempered child everyone at Poore Pond knew him to be and held no ill will against the school or anyone there, least of all David.

But the boy's parents were divided. Mr. Barrett did not hold the school responsible and felt that the entire situation was handled as well as it could have been.

Mrs. Barrett; however, was poised to file a lawsuit against the school board, Dr. Fleming, Joe Maynor, and David's parents. She told Dr. Fleming that she would be withdrawing her son from school as soon as she could organize what she needed to home school him.

David was another story. He spent every possible moment with Julian, spending time at his house after school most days. David's parents agreed that he could invite Julian to their house, but Mrs. Barrett would not allow it. She was still in her ready-to-sue frame of mind.

Hope, suppressing this-would-not-have-happened-on-Ray's-watch thoughts, sent for Joe Maynor. She wanted first, to console him as best she could and second, to help him understand regulations mandated by the board for using student helpers.

Remembering the trigger for the board's revising old regulations on student helpers, Hope shuddered. A six-year-old was killed when a folding table—much like the one that injured Julian—fell on a boy named Jarod and fractured his skull. It had happened a few years ago in another district; and the State's response was to pass *Jarod's Law,*[9] filled with an extensive list of new—many unrelated—health and safety regulations.

As uncomfortable as it was for both of them, Hope shared this background with Joe.

"Actually, I asked David to help me with the folded table, meaning to control the move myself with a little muscle from him." Joe said, his face ashen, eyes troubled.

"But David, the self-starter that he is, got right on it before I knew what he was doing." He pounded the side of his head with his fist.

"No, don't keep beating yourself up, Joe," Hope said, patting his arm. "It just happened. It was an accident."

Joe sighed heavily and looked out the window at the courtyard.

Neither spoke for several moments.

"You know, Hope, I work mostly at the high schools. We use those big kids all the time. No one ever told me it was against board policy."

"Those secondary kids are a bit different, Joe," Hope said. "They are not as vulnerable as our little elementary students. We cannot use our students for very heavy lifting or moving."

She handed him a thick packet of paper. "Here is a copy of the revised policy. You will want to study it."

"There's a rumor going round that Julian's parents are set to sue me. Do you know anything about that, Hope?" Joe's voice went thin.

"No, I don't. I've heard rumors of lawsuits against all of us, but I have no idea if they're true," Hope said, rising.

She dismissed Joe with a handshake and thanked him for coming. *I will find a way to eliminate those folding tables altogether,* she told herself.

Finally getting to her email, Hope found a message from Holly Hapwell.

> The parent group has heard about Mr. Taylor's
> accident, and we want to help him and his
> family.
> What do you think would be useful? We've
> been taking home-cooked meals to his house
> but want to do more. His wife is obviously
> overwhelmed.
> She seems quite dazed. Would a spaghetti
> supper or some other kind of benefit be
> appropriate?
> Please advise.

No wonder Felice seems dazed; she's facing criminal charges for spousal abuse and her marriage has fallen apart, Hope thought. But of course the parents don't know all that—not yet.

A second email, a copy of that sent by Chuck to the teachers' association president and copied to Desiree Osmond, stated his resignation as building co-representative, due to medical leave and the long recuperation period he faced.

Brad Kushner came to Hope's office well after dismissal to inform her of plans the teachers had for supporting their colleague. Brad had already begun to help Chuck find an apartment since he expected to be released in a matter of weeks.

"It has to be a first-floor unit, preferably near the hospital," Brad said. "His therapy will be provided in the hospital's physical-therapy center, and the doctors say it will take more than a year at best."

"Does Chuck have any family, Brad?" Hope asked. "Do you know?"

"He told me he has only an ailing father in the Vancouver area and an estranged brother, God knows where."

Brad turned away. His voice thick, he said, "We're the only family he has now. He can't work. He can't go out on his own." He looked at Hope, bravely exposing his compassionate face, "And he has to deal with the fact that his wife practically killed him."

He stepped to the window and gazed into the courtyard. "On top of that, he's dealing with legal proceedings against Felice."

Facing Hope again, he asked, "Did you know she has a black belt in karate and is accomplished in judo? By law, such skills are lethal weapons, I've heard." He shook his head.

Hope asked to be included in the sign-up sheets for dollar donations and supplies to Chuck's apartment as well as volunteering time to help.

~ ~ ~

Walking into PolyFlem felt strange. Hope was glad she had seen Michael face-to-face recently, somewhat warming their icy, long-estranged relationship.

The fact that Michael was actually hosting the Saturday open breakfast for the hungry completely amazed her. Could Brooke be having an influence on him, she asked herself. Or is it George? Of course, it's George.

Smells of fresh coffee and bacon frying filled the building; Hope followed her nose down a wide corridor to a vast manufacturing floor.

Equipment and materials lined the walls; some areas were curtained off, others blocked with yellow police tape.

Long folding tables with chairs were placed at right angles in the center of the expanse. Propane cooktops on wheels stood near a separate table covered with food and utensils.

Michael and George worked chef duty while Brooke arranged stacks of plates.

"Well here's Dr. Hope," Michael called to her. "What would you like? We have time to catch a little breakfast before the customers come." Brooke waved at her.

George brought a plate of scrambled eggs with cheese and crispy bacon. He brought also, a huge smile and a hug. Brooke came with steaming coffee.

The four of them enjoyed an amiable, quick breakfast, Michael and Brooke on one side of the table, Hope and George opposite them. They reminded each other of last-minute details in preparation for their guests.

Hope was struck by the wonder of it all. Noting the large quantities of food, coffee, juice—even fresh bagels and donuts, she was impressed by the way Michael had really stepped up for this cause. It looked as if he had spared no expense.

A throng of partakers arrived, and suddenly a flurry of activity began. Several shelter residents appeared and immediately pitched in wherever needed.

Hope was in charge of beverages. She tried to keep ahead of requests with rows of filled coffee mugs and large glasses of orange juice, but they disappeared rapidly. Some guests requested tea or hot chocolate, so she poured hot water from an electric urn into cups with powdered hot-chocolate mix or teabags.

The families bringing children for breakfast—though few in number—saddened her.

"Two hot chocolates, please," a small voice spoke to Hope's back as she dug in a box for more teabags. She turned and saw a familiar child standing before her.

"Dwayne," she said. "Do you recognize me, Dwayne Hickerson?" She was taken aback to see a Poore Pond student.

"Yes, I recognize you, Dr. Fleming," he smiled. "You're the principal at my school. You taught our math class that day when Mrs. Newhouse got sick and had to go home."

"That's right, Dwayne," she said, remembering both the incident and how unusually articulate the boy had been even as a kindergartner. "Who's here with you?"

"My mom," he said, gesturing toward the food table. "I'll go get her." He dashed off before Hope could object.

Feeling embarrassed for Mrs. Hickerson, she prepared the two hot chocolates Dwayne had requested, while searching for the right matter-of-fact-but-sensitive words to say in this delicate situation. I think she had a good job. Was it in health care?

Mother and son approached the drinks table, both smiling, Dwayne genuinely, his mother artificially.

"It's good to see you, Mrs. Hickerson," she said, meaning it and trying to keep her eyes from searching the woman's face.

"Surprised to see me here, aren't you?" she asked Hope.

"Well, of course I am," Hope said softly. "What—

"Not as surprised as I am to find myself here," she interrupted.

Touching her son's shoulder, she said, "Dwayne, please take the hot chocolates to the table where I put our plates. I'll be right there." He did as she told him.

"Are you looking for a place to live, Mrs. Hickerson?" Hope asked.

"Oh no, we're still living with my mom like always. But I've been laid off from my job—for five months now." She looked over toward Dwayne sitting at a table, already tucking into a plate of food. "We're a little strapped for cash right now, so we ended up here today," she said with a brave face. "Got out of Mom's hair."

"Every little bit helps, doesn't it?" Hope said.

"Every little bit helps," Mrs. Hickerson said. "And I have a job interview on Monday. I should be back at work soon."

Hope filled three large Styrofoam containers with food, putting them neatly into a plastic shopping bag. At the last moment, she added several packets of hot chocolate and teabags. Then she threw a handful of sugar packets in as well and looked around for other possibilities.

She saw the Hickerson's approaching the door and hurried to give them the bag. They thanked her quietly and turned to go.

"Mrs. Hickerson, is Dwayne in the lunch program?"

She shook her head no, her eyes questioning.

"I'll send the form home, so you can look at it. He would probably qualify for either free or reduced-price lunches, which would apply to school-supply fees as well. Good luck, Mrs. Hickerson. Goodbye, Dwayne." She waved to the little family, her heart bleeding for them.

I remember now. Mrs. Hickerson ran the lab at City Hospital, having been promoted to manager several years ago. It was quite a big responsibility—and a good salary.

Whom do I know in hospital administration?

Hope excused herself from clean-up duties and left PolyFlem feeling good about the success of Michael's first breakfast. She stifled all thoughts of the Hickerson's plight.

On the drive home, her cell phone rang but stopped as she dug with one hand for it in her purse.

She pulled happily into the driveway at the Canterbury Road house and immediately felt comforted. She sat in the car a moment and checked the missed call.

It was Bernard McElson with no real news, just a request for her to go through Mary Baldwin's papers. He'd been all through them and found nothing further to fend off Franklin. But since she had more familiarity with Mary's spidery handwriting as well as the person Mary, perhaps she could catch even a line or two that would shed light on her intent. It was worth a try.

Not up to a phone conversation with Bernard, she simply typed him a short text message. Will do. Talk Mon.

She entered the house with a heavy heart. I don't really want to face those papers, she told herself. I am not up to all that guilt.

Chapter Seventeen
Ray

Ray, lacking his usual confidence because of allegations against him, nervously rang the doorbell at the Barrett house. From seeing her at school, he recognized Julian's mother when she opened the door.

"Yes?" she said, unsmiling but with eyes warm. "Oh, you're the famous Mr. Sellers, from Poore Pond School, aren't you?"

Ray felt heat rising up his neck and swallowed. What does she think I'm famous for, he wondered. Fiona had been able to keep the case out of the media so far.

"That's me—I guess," he said, managing a phony smile. "I'm Ray Sellers, but I don't know about the famous part."

"Mr. Sellers!" Julian appeared, grinning widely. He opened the storm door. "Come in. It's all right, isn't it, Mom?"

"See what I mean about the famous part?" Mrs. Barrett laughed, stepping aside for him to enter. "I assume you heard what happened to Julian."

"I did. I did. That's why I'm here," Ray said. "I hated hearing it." He looked at the boy. "How are you feeling, Julian? What's that headgear you're wearing?"

"Okay," Julian said. "Better now that you're here." Like two magnets, their hands met in a warm handshake. "The doctor wants me to wear this thing for a few weeks." His fingers brushed the half-helmet.

Mrs. Barrett led them to the living room. "Sit down," she said. "I'll get cold drinks."

"All the kids miss you at school," Julian said, still smiling. "Mr. Maynor's okay, but he's not used to kids our age. He came from the high school."

"I told you you were famous, Mr. Sellers," Mrs. Barrett appeared with three glasses of iced tea on a tray. "All the Poore Pond children know who you are; you touch them."

"Touch them?" Ray asked, hypersensitive given the circumstances but knowing she did not mean it the wrong way.

"Touch them, touch their hearts. You know, win them over," she said, embarrassing herself. "You connect with them."

Now he knew he was blushing. "You're so nice, thanks," Ray said, looking toward her but unable to meet her gaze. "Actually, it's the kids who touch my heart," he said, eyes serious, voice low.

He stayed another half hour and played a video game with Julian. All the while, he could not help wondering if this nice mother was really planning to sue everybody over her son's accident. She did not seem the type to do that.

When it was time to go, Julian and his mother gave Ray a big hug and thanked him for coming. The boy walked him to his car and gave him another hug, making Ray uncomfortable. He spotted the package he had forgotten on the front seat. He pulled it out and handed it to Julian. The child opened it in an instant, breaking all gift-opening speed records Ray had ever seen. The bag of Tootsie Rolls and set of trading cards thrilled him.

"Thank you so much, Mr. Sellers," he said, offering his hand in a grown-up way. They shook hands formally. "Will you come see me again?" he asked.

On the drive home, Ray reviewed every minute of the visit. It was clear that it had meant a great deal to Julian and also to his mother, who could not have been more welcoming.

If she had known the charges against me, would she have been as nice, he thought. I doubt it. I took a big chance going there. Fiona would have my head.

He called Heather from his cell phone. She sounded unusually tired.

"Will you stop for pizza, Ray?' She sighed. He could picture her rubbing her temples. "I was going to make chicken a' la king—you know—over toast. But I'm all-in."

"Would you like me to make the chicken on toast?" he asked, wanting the family to have a home-cooked meal.

"If you want to, Ray. But I've already promised Jeremy pepperoni pizza."

"We'll have both, Heather. You rest."

Just after supper, Claire and Leonard dropped in, full of exuberance about a list.

"What list is that, Claire?" Ray asked, wiping the last countertop. "Heather's resting. Let's keep quiet."

Claire explained the fact that Hope and she had started a list of people they would ask to write reference letters in her brother's behalf.

"Whose idea was that?" he asked.

"Hope said it will come down to that; so when Fiona asks, we'll be ready." She dug in her purse. "We already have quite a few names."

"You haven't asked anyone yet have you?" Ray questioned, thoroughly uncomfortable with the entire idea.

"It's better to be proactive, Ray," Leonard said, scrutinizing Jeremy's football cards spread out on the coffee table. "Where's Jeremy?"

"He went to basketball practice with his friend," Ray said.

Claire showed him the list, counting down the names. There were seventeen, mostly all from school. Ray had a fleeting thought about Mrs. Barrett. Would she write me a character reference, he wondered then thought better of it.

The guests left early, promising to add to the list of names.

"Thanks for stopping, Claire. You, too, Leonard," Ray said, meaning it.

"This is getting to be a habit," Leonard laughed, giving Claire his arm as they started down the steep steps. "Thanks."

"But don't contact anyone about a letter yet," Ray called.

Jeremy arrived home and immediately went to prepare for bed. He appeared in pajamas, carrying his spelling workbook.

"Ray, will you give my words to me, please. The test is tomorrow."

"Sure, Sport," he said, welcoming the distraction. He liked helping the boy practice for his spelling tests. They had a routine. First, Ray would say the words, and Jeremy would spell them orally. Then he would have him make up sentences, using the words correctly.

When a particular word lent itself to humor, Jeremy made the sentences funny; and they would giggle and build even funnier related sentences. This would send them rolling in laughter.

Finally, there would be a written test. If Jeremy had ninety to one-hundred percent correct, Ray gave him one dollar. It was difficult to tell who enjoyed the game more.

After tucking the boy into bed, Ray went to see Heather, resting in the bedroom. He put his hand on her forehead, and she opened her eyes.

"I think I'm here for the night, Ray," she said sleepily. "I hope you don't mind."

"No, you rest, Heather," he said, stroking her hand. "I'm just going to look over Fiona's papers for awhile. I won't be long."

Reluctantly, he pulled a pack of papers from yet another envelope his lawyer had sent over in the name of keeping him informed. *If I have to read more long descriptions of Tommy Grant's charges against me, I'm going to heave,* he thought.

But these were police reports of Josh Wentworth's accusation against the soccer coach—a Will James—and also against the step-grandfather, Raymond Snell.

There were marked similarities in the two statements the boy had given. In both cases, Josh said he had been molested in the alleged perpetrators' cars. And that it happened while they were driving him home. He claimed that both men had specifically asked him to sit in the front seat. *That little punk sure covers all his bases.*

When asked where the incidents happened, Josh said it was on Reservoir Road, a dark and shadowy, two-lane, rural road. He described feeling fearful when he realized he was being taken the wrong way to his house. In both cases? With two different so-called molesters? Ray was skeptical.

A light went on in his mind when he vaguely recalled hearing Fiona make these points at one of their meetings. But he had been too overwhelmed to absorb any of it at the time.

He went to the desk, pulled out his own folder on the case, and retrieved a copy of Tommy Grant's statement, written in typical thirteen-year-old writing, part manuscript-part cursive.

Tommy claimed the molestation had occurred in his bedroom while he was trying to play a video game, and Mr. Sellers was waiting for the father to come home. No pattern here, Ray noted.

Tommy then stated that it had also happened before they reached his house, quietly, in the front seat of the car while Josh rode in the back. There's Josh's pattern, Ray thought.

Continuing, Ray winced when he read Tommy's further claim that it had happened prior to that night, behind the dumpster at Poore Pond School. On various occasions.

Where have I been? Ray asked himself, pounding the side of his head with his fist. But he knew, until now, he had been too horrified from the shameful accusations to take in the details.

It's time to quit licking my wounds, he thought. Fiona wants me hopping mad, and now I'm ready to fight.

He dialed his attorney's number. She answered on the first ring. Ray started right in desecrating the statements of both boys and agreeing with Fiona that Josh's stories definitely informed Tommy's.

"Well, congratulations Ray!" she exclaimed. "Poor-Little-Victim-Ray is gone." He could hear her exhale. "Fight-to-the-Death-for-his-Honor-Ray has finally arrived. Now you're ready to really help me defend you."

"I have been all along," Ray whined.

"Are you kidding?" she said. "Up to now, I've been doing all the heavy lifting. It's time you did some of the work."

"Be at my office at eight forty-five sharp tomorrow morning, Fighter Ray. We are ready to strategize, big time. I love this part."

Ray heard the dial tone.

Chapter Eighteen
The Bradfords

After the fifth telephone call produced a parent willing to trade the clean-up shift for the early one serving the Valentine breakfast, Helsi sighed with relief.

What was I thinking when I told Mary Cartwright I would fill in for her at seven, with the hectic mornings at this house? And poor Ian, she continued to berate herself, *should not be expected to put her volunteer duties ahead of his professional obligations. I can be such a nincompoop.*

Ian was right when he said I need to be smarter about managing my business time, she thought. *But I need to be smarter about family time, too. When Mercedes comes to stay with us, I will need to be super smart,* she thought.

She hurried upstairs. "Ian," she said, watching him button his shirt. "Our problem is solved—well, my problem. Susan Clay volunteered her husband for the early shift this morning."

"That poor schmuck," Ian said humorlessly. "Helsi, you mean you actually had the nerve to call people before six a.m.?"

"I know which ones are early risers," she said feebly.

"You also know your family priorities—deep down you do," he said, gathering his keys and coins from the dresser top.

Thoughts of Mercedes dominated her mind as she cleared the breakfast table. She placed the last bowl in the dishwasher, closed and sealed the door, and turned the switch.

Helsi found herself at the computer, Googling *Munchausen by Proxy Syndrome*. She had to understand the nature of the illness for Mercedes' sake. If she secretly resented Phyllis, it would come out in subtle ways, confusing the child. And for my sake, she thought; resentment can destroy you.

What had Phyllis done to Mercedes? Herb told Ian that she'd been "doing things" to make Mercedes sick, that she could have killed her.

Frantic to know more, Helsi scrolled through the endless list, settling on a Wikipedia site. An article from the renowned Cleveland Clinic described MPS as "a type of factitious disorder, a mental illness in which a person acts as if an individual he or she is caring for has a physical or mental illness when the person is not really sick." [10]

Were all those hospitalizations unnecessary, she questioned. But I know Mercedes was really sick that night Phyllis brought her here. I saw the evidence; I smelled it.

She read further and froze at these words: "*…might create or exaggerate the child's symptoms…might simply lie about symptoms…or induce symptoms through various means, such as poisoning, suffocating, starving, and causing infection.*"

Mercedes was having excessive vomiting and diarrhea that night. Helsi recalled that she had wanted to wash and change the child before paramedics took her away, but Ian urged her to leave it to hospital staff. Did he see her soil as evidence? It bothered me for days afterward that I had not done that for Mercedes.

Create or induce symptoms, poisoning?

She abruptly closed the website and logged off the internet. That poor child, she mourned.

Unable to bear the thought of what Mercedes went through, she hurried downstairs. It was nearly time to leave for the middle school.

She actually enjoyed cleaning up. The breakfast had been a huge success, and she could see that Lucy was proud of her for volunteering. She popped into the kitchen afterward with two classmates, clearly showing off her mother.

Hope enjoyed the other volunteers. Everyone worked hard and laughed harder, joking sarcastically about working like slaves to give their brilliant children a bit of royal treatment. The camaraderie made the job fun.

On the drive home, Helsi put it all into perspective. Here I am earning volunteer points by cleaning at school. Next I will clean our home to earn the family's love. Tonight I will clean offices to earn income. Cleaning is my life. She smiled at the thought.

She quickly vacuumed the living room and stairway, removed fingerprints from walls and door frames, and prepared a pan of stuffed cabbages for Lucy to put in the oven.

Lucy has been keeping everything together well on Wednesday nights, Helsi thought. The children get a good dinner, baths and to bed on time; and the kitchen is tidy when I get home. She is certainly earning the bit of money I pay her.

There was just enough time to mix and bake a batch of chocolate-chunk squares before Ian would come wanting lunch. He would be famished and would need more than the leftover chicken- dumpling soup she planned to serve. So she prepared small chopped salads and grilled-cheese-with-ham sandwiches.

Even if I land enough new accounts to hire another person, I should keep doing the Wednesday night jobs myself; so Lucy can keep her responsibilities and her pocket money.

Wind whistled around the house, causing drafts at the back door and chilling the kitchen. Still mindful of her decision to pamper Ian more, she turned on the gas logs in the living-room fireplace. She unfolded a card table and placed it before the fire, covering it with a clean tablecloth.

The table was set for lunch when Ian arrived, and the aroma of baked cookies filled the house.

"What is this?" he asked, smiling broadly. "Are we celebrating something?" He washed his hands at the sink.

"Just lunch, Ian," she said, taking his hand and leading him to the table. "Just lunch and just life with your nicer wife."

Ian thought of the phone call he'd had from Herb. It was a different sort of Herb—more forceful, almost demanding. He had outlined specific dates and instructions for Mercedes' move to their home and into their care, covering legal aspects Ian had not yet considered.

He decided not to tell Helsi now. It would spoil this lovely lunch she had put so much work into preparing. They could discuss it when she was home Friday night.

Ian told another of his clinic-patient stories while they finished their salads. "I am learning so much about the psychology of treating patients in pain, Helsi," he said, handing his empty plate to her.

She returned with sandwiches and soup then refilled his glass of iced tea before sitting down again.

"Are patients in pain so different from other patients, Ian?" she asked, blowing on the steaming soup to cool it.

"This is really good, Hon," he said alternating bites of sandwich with spoonfuls of soup. "Yes. Yes they are," he said. "Many of them—most of them—are in such dire pain that it's an ordeal just to get on the doctor's table and be examined."

"The crotchety old ones, you mean?" she asked.

"Is there more soup?" Ian asked, holding out his bowl.

"Of course," she said, getting it for him. She placed the refilled bowl before him and sat down again.

"This fire feels so good after that drafty kitchen." She took a tiny bite of sandwich and looked at her husband. "What were you saying about grumpy old patients?"

"That's just it, Helsi," he looked squarely in her eyes. "They aren't all old. We had three younger ones—probably not a day over thirty-eight or -nine in one case and early forties in the other two."

He pushed his plate to the side and helped himself to a chocolate-chunk square from the platter. His wife poured coffee from the carafe for both of them.

"What sort of pain do they have? They're too young for arthritis."

Ian gave a brief account of their chronic, pain-inflicting conditions but spoke in paragraphs about ways he has learned to handle them carefully and respectfully. He wanted Helsi to know that these patients are in, not only physical pain, but also emotional and mental pain from being so incapacitated.

"Pain—if severe enough—can bring down even a big, strapping, forty-something ex-marine," he said, empathy filling his face.

He had much more to say. She gave her all to listening attentively. But Helsi, anxious for him to finish, was bursting to tell him her latest business decision.

Apparently having said everything he meant to, Ian turned his chair to the fire and stretched his legs toward it. "This is really nice, Hon," he said, glancing at his watch. "And don't think I haven't noticed all you've been doing lately." His eyes met hers. "You should find a way to have more time at home; it suits you." He smiled affectionately at her.

"That's what I wanted to tell you," she said, returning the smile.

"Oh—I almost forgot, Helsi," he interrupted. "Dr. Joe wants you to call him. He's looking for a new office cleaner, hasn't been happy with the one he has now."

"Perfect," she said, giggling. She came and sat on his lap. "I was going to say that I wanted to get more accounts and hire another person. If I cost the new jobs right, I could afford to work less and be home more."

"I'd like that," Ian said.

"I'd like that," Helsi echoed.

Especially with another child to care for, he thought, not wanting to broach the subject of Mercedes just yet.

I have a feeling that Mercedes is going to be high maintenance—emotionally, that is, Helsi silently anticipated. If we agree to take her in, she thought, pretending that they had not yet made a commitment to Herb.

When Ian and Helsi finally sat down together to discuss—without their offspring—actually caring for Mercedes, they each had specific ideas that had been forming in their minds for weeks.

"We need another bedroom," Helsi said matter-of-factly.

"Exactly," Ian confirmed. "It wouldn't take much to convert that attic space above the garage into a bedroom." He reached for a pad of paper and pencil.

"We just need to bring a heating and cooling duct into that room, put up drywall, and paint it." He sketched a diagram showing how to extend the unused duct in the garage straight up to the attic room above, and showed it to Helsi.

"But you were hoping for a heated garage someday, Ian. That's why the duct was put in, remember? It was one of the reasons you wanted to buy this house in the first place."

"Oh, we never did make it operational, Helsi," he said. "And now we have a better use for it."

They agreed to get estimates the next day. Herb was due to report to the job in Belgium late March or early April. That was six weeks from now at the most.

But when they told the children, Sean's face fell. Lucy and Rachel wanted to know who would have the new room.

"You know I've needed a room of my own since forever. I'll be in high school in two years, and I'm still bunking with my baby sister!" Lucy moaned. Rachel looked hurt.

Robbie and Dylan glanced at one another and smiled sheepishly. They were perfectly happy in a bedroom together.

"You promised me I could move into that room in the basement when I got older. Remember?" Sean stood and slapped his hands on his hips. "Hello! I am older now. Let's move me down there this second. I could have all my stuff in there in half a day." He smiled at the idea.

Ian and Helsi looked at one another with wide eyes. Ian hugged Sean.

"What?" he asked, looking suspiciously at his dad.

"Thanks for a great idea, son."

"Sean's way would be much simpler," Helsi said. "Not to mention cheaper and faster."

"Why not do both?" Lucy asked, sitting down on the arm of her mother's chair. "Then Mercedes could have the new room, and I would settle for Sean's old room." Her face was full of nobility.

"But I want Mercedes in my room with me," Rachel whined. "We should not leave her alone at night with no mommy and daddy."

Ian found her compassion heartwarming and gave her a loving smile. *Is she the only Bradford child not thinking of herself?*

In the end, the family agreed that Sean would move into the basement; and Lucy would take his old room, finally getting her privacy. Mercedes would share with Rachel.

Later, without the children present, the parents decided they would need to purchase only a few pieces of furniture for Lucy and perhaps a rug for Sean.

They also discussed ways to make Mercedes feel, not only at home, but also part of the family. They would help her keep honorable thoughts of her mother and regular communication with both parents. Emails to Herb and letters to Phyllis would be encouraged.

House rules for the Bradford children would apply to Mercedes as well. Disputes would be handled with loving adjudication.

"There will be disputes," Ian said. "Once they start, we will know that Mercedes considers herself a part of our family." His eyes sought Helsi's. "It won't be easy for us."

"It won't be easy for Mercedes," she added. "She's a smart girl; she's bound to know what's going on with Phyllis. And who knows what she writes to her daughter in those sweet little notes Herb said she keeps sending."

They lay in bed thinking noble thoughts.

I hope Mercedes' health holds up, Ian thought. *She could have long-term effects from all those drugs Phyllis must have given her. We don't even know how sick or well she's actually been.*

Rachel can be bossy and territorial. I hope she doesn't start to resent Mercedes' taking over half her room, Helsi contemplated. *What are we getting ourselves into?*

Chapter Nineteen
Hope

"Nothing jumps out from these ledgers, Hope," Theo said closing another and placing it on the stack. "I don't really know what I'm looking for, but they seem to be in good order."

Hope put aside a file of documents and looked at the discarded ledger, noting the date on the cover: 1979. I started working for Mary in—let's see…mid '79, she searched her memory.

She glanced at Theo, already halfway through the 1980 green binder. He did not look up.

It was in June of the next year that I began keeping Mary's books, she remembered, heart pounding.

And it was November of 1980—that fateful day-that I committed my first felonious act. She coughed to relieve her dry mouth and reached for the wine goblet.

"It's interesting to see how Mrs. Baldwin disbursed her money," Theo said, eyes on the page.

She tried to will guilty feelings off her face and looked at him with dispassionate eyes. Her stomach churned. "How so?" she asked, her voice off pitch.

"Well, four hundred dollars to Madame Bovinsky? This shows up every few months." He looked at her without seeing before lowering his eyes back to the page.

Hope recalled the pretentious astrologist Mary consulted.

"And this one, five thousand dollars every month to Hope Ministries—wasn't that a big evangelist group on television and radio in the seventies or eighties? Wow! They must have prayed their hearts out for Mary Baldwin," Theo said in disbelief.

Not five-thousand dollars every month, Hope said to herself, wanting—but not wanting—to reveal her entire deceitful scheme to him. She said nothing.

Every so often, she checked to see what year Theo was on in the ledger stack. Her pulse raced each time. She continued perusing letters in the file, suddenly noticing that each one bore a small, square label with a number on it, fixed to the upper right margin. She leafed back through to see if they were chronological, which they were.

There must be a cross-referencing system, she thought and reached for a ledger. She turned many pages before finding a small, precise numeral written in black-felt pen next to a cheque entry. Should I send Theo to 1981, the year my illicit deeds began, she asked herself. He already knows I have an unprosecuted felony in my past.

"Theo," she said softly. In the moment it took him to look up at her, she lost the will to let him in on the whole story. "Theo, are you at all hungry? It's been hours since we ate."

"Only slightly, Hope." He smiled at her. "We should finish this so you can be rid of it. Why? Are you?"

"Not really," she said and reached for ledger 1981. What she found astonished her. Not in ledger 1981, but in ledger 1982, next to an entry for a cheque made out to Hope Minster she found inscribed, a small, black numeral: #5 - 247. Hope checked the front of the file folder, the contents of which she was now reviewing, and found it labeled: #2. She found that the letters and papers it held were numbered 51 – 100.

She put it all out of her mind when Theo pronounced the entire search finished and they broke for supper. She did not think of it again until she lay in bed that night unable to sleep.

Wrapping a fleece robe around her, she went straight to the study and pulled file folder #5 from the box. In the space where document #247 should have been was a blank sheet of paper with a notation on it:

Item #247 in green envelope in safety deposit box.

She had to see Item #247. *I'll call Bernard tomorrow,* she told herself as she climbed the stairs to bed.

Hope took the binder on her bedside table and settled on the pillows to review the research on teaching phonics. She had scheduled a special meeting on reading instruction for primary teachers next week.

She knew that if she got into intense reading of meaty subject matter so late at night, she would start her juices flowing and be unable to sleep at all. Still, she plodded through the pages.

Something drastic had to be done about plummeting fourth-grade comprehension scores. A discussion of implicit and explicit phonics really caught her attention.

> *Primary children are taught to read by decoding beginning and ending letter sounds along with using sentence context and picture cues—even guesses—to read whole words. Since primary-grade stories have controlled vocabularies and many pictures, most children succeed with this method.*

This traditional approach is now called *implicit phonics,* she thought.

"Humph," Hope said aloud. "That's a new term to me."

But what really got her attention was an excerpt from a New York Times article describing:

> *…epidemic numbers of pharmacists misreading prescriptions by confusing words like chlorpromazine (an antipsychotic) with chlorpropramine (lowers blood sugar) with sometimes fatal results. These words begin and end with the same letters and have the same general shape.* [11]

She immediately recalled often-used, reading-readiness lessons on word configuration. *We had them doing all that finger* tracing of words written in sandpaper letters, so very young children would notice the shapes of words. She sat up, sighed, and looked into space.

"Some teachers even had young children forming words in sand with their tiny fingers," she said to the walls. And recalled how every primary classroom had to have an expensive sand table.

Hope finished reading the argument for using *explicit phonics* to prevent the "fourth-grade slump in reading achievement" and closed the binder. It's worth a try, she thought as she turned off the light.

Snuggling under the quilts, she vowed to read further research.

The telephone rang sharply. Hope answered it, expecting Joe Maynor from school.

"Good morning, Mom," George's delightful voice resonated in her ear.

"George, it's five forty-five in the morning. What on earth is the matter?"

"Oh nothing's the matter, Mom. I just wanted to hear your voice."

"Aren't you sweet," Hope murmured. "But what do you really need other than to check your charm meter?"

"Charm meter, that's good, Mom. Did I make my usual high score?" They laughed.

"Do you think the shelter could give Uncle Mark a job?" he asked, his voice serious now. "Until he gets on his feet."

"Has he recuperated enough to work, George? His surgery was just a few months ago, wasn't it?"

"Two months. But I was thinking maybe a desk job or something. While he's still recuperating," George said, his voice full of compassion. "He needs something to do, you know, Mom?"

Neither spoke for a moment.

"And he needs money," George added softly.

Hope, sleep deprived and minus her morning cup of tea, had no ideas at the moment.

She promised to think about a job Mark might do and confer with Theo, too. She would get back to him.

She sat at the counter sipping steamy tea and considered the day ahead. She had not stopped thinking about the green envelope, Item #247, in a safety deposit box and was anxious to ring Bernard and get her hands on it.

The telephone rang again. This time it was Ray Sellers informing her that she would be receiving a letter from Fiona Fitzenrider, asking her to be a character witness for him.

"Of course, Ray," she said softly. "Is there anything else I can do for you?"

"No thanks, Hope. Being a character witness is enough to ask you to do."

"How is that going, Ray?" she asked softly.

"I think it's going good," he said. "I have a crackerjack lawyer and the plaintiff has a weak case. It's going good." They said their good-byes.

Hope replaced the telephone with a smile. Ray sounded really upbeat, she thought. He sounded too assertive to be Ray Sellers. That can only help him fight.

But she dreaded the day the entire story would be on the front page of the newspaper. Even if Ray is found innocent of the charges, much damage will have already been done. There will be pressure to fire him.

Chapter Twenty
Ray

Ray sat across the table from Fiona and sweated profusely. He looked around her office. "Could we open a window, Fiona? I'm about to sweat to death."

"It's not the room temperature, Ray; it's the subject matter with which we're dealing." She looked up from her papers. "Your adrenalin is racing and overheating you. But that's good."

He stood, running his finger inside his collar. He loosened his tie.

"Go ahead, Ray. Remove your jacket," Fiona ordered.

Ray slipped out of his blazer and looked around for a place to put it. He hung it on a coat rack near the door.

"That's better," he said, seating himself.

"Okay, Ray. Describe the seating order in the car that night one more time, please," Fiona said.

"Fiona, I've told you a hundred times. I put all three boys in the back seat, just as Hope advised me," Ray said impatiently.

"What did she tell you?" Fiona asked

"She said, 'Always be aware of your proximity to a child. You must protect yourself at all times against false accusations. There are—not many, but a few—paranoid parents out there who would rather hurt you than have their children or themselves exposed.'" He looked into space, remembering their discussions.

"Hope is a wise woman," Fiona said smiling. "And you are a wise man to have taken her advice. Unfortunately, both Josh and Tommy stated that Tommy sat in the front seat with you."

"Well, they're lying," Ray said, his voice rising. "What about Andrew? What did he say?"

"Mrs. Billings refuses to let me question him. And since he's only six-years-old, I cannot subpoena him." Fiona said.

"But you can easily discredit Josh's word with all his history of accusing people, can't you, Fiona-The-Hotshot-Attorney?"

"Stop smirking, Ray. Of course I can dishonor Josh's testimony." Fiona stared through him. "But Tommy is another matter."

Ray pounded his fist on the table and cursed. "This has to be settled soon; it has to," he demanded. "My wife's poor health is getting worse. My son has forgotten how to be a good boy. I'll be lucky to keep my job even after I win the case."

Ray's last point thrilled Fiona, but she did not comment.

He's mad and full of fight, but he's still certain he will prevail, she thought. What could be better?

They broke for lunch and made it a point to get away from each other. Fiona went to her club, and Ray went to Cheeseburger Palace.

While waiting for his order, he texted Heather that things were going great and asked about her energy level. When his sandwich was half consumed, his phone signaled a text message:

If things are going great there, I feel great.

He swallowed hard and left without finishing his lunch, walking back through a small park. It was warm for March. He checked his watch and sat down on a bench under a pergola.

His mind filed through the events of the night he drove the boys home. He replayed every scene over and over, from the minute the three boys climbed into his back seat to Mr. Grant's coming through the door of his house.

Little Andrew knows the truth, he thought. How can I get Mrs. Billings to help us? Mrs. Billings. She treated me like scum for returning her son even though she was at fault, not knowing where her six-year-old was after dark.

Mrs. Billings. Mrs. Billings. A small grin spread across Ray's lips. She watched Tommy get out of the back seat to let Andrew out, he recalled. She saw all three boys in the back seat.

Ray could see the scene in his mind's eye: Andrew had started to climb over Tommy; and Tommy stepped out like a gentleman, impressing Ray. Mrs. Billings had stood in the driveway watching and scowling at everyone.

Fiona and Ray reconvened; he told her of his revelation.

"I will pay a call to Mrs. Billings this afternoon, Ray. Good work. But first we have a few more points to dissect." She smiled.

Another two hours passed before Fiona was finished with Ray. She sat back and praised him for his contributions to the case.

"I always knew it was there inside you, Ray," she said.

Ray thought immediately of Bluewave's class motto, *It's there inside you.* He looked into space. She was right. It is there inside us. Ability we never knew we had. Fight we never knew we had. He looked at Fiona.

"I knew you were capable of recalling details and analyzing them for evidence value." Fiona said. "Some—most—people do not move into fighting mode until they've gone through a dreamlike disbelief phase. When it finally sinks in that they're up against very high stakes, anger builds and adrenalin rises."

She stood and Ray joined her.

"So I'm right on schedule?" he asked.

"You are right on schedule." They laughed together. "And we have a trial date, Ray. May twenty-fourth." She extended her hand. Ray gave her a warm grip then left the office.

Chapter Twenty-One
The Bradfords

"Mom, Mercedes wants pancakes for breakfast," Robbie wailed when Helsi set plates of scrambled eggs with cheese on the table.

"No, Robbie, I don't," Mercedes said softly, clearly embarrassed.

"You said!" Robbie insisted. "You said you missed your mom's pancakes." He looked accusingly at her.

"Mercedes Sweetie," Helsi said, locking eyes with the girl. "We'll have pancakes this weekend." She handed her a fork. "Are pancakes your favorite breakfast?"

The child lowered her eyes and nodded.

Robbie opened his mouth to speak but felt his mother's burning stare and uttered not a word.

Rachel scooted her chair closer to Mercedes' and offered her a triangle of toast. Smiling appreciatively, her friend grasped the small gift carefully.

Later, Helsi spent the morning tidying the house and obsessively reviewing Mercedes' behavior the eight days she had been under the Bradford roof. Things had gone relatively smoothly, for the most part.

The children—except for Rachel—had gone about their business unbothered by the child's presence, making it a point to express warm greetings or quiet jokes to her in passing, some even giving her small tokens of affection. Sean gave her a lava light from his old room. Robbie and Dylan donated a small, stuffed Curious George and a set of his storybooks to her side of the bookshelf in Rachel's room.

The smiling, joyful Mercedes they had seen on visits with her parents was nowhere to be found. But she quietly followed house rules and routines without complaint.

Allowing Snowball to become a housecat had been a smart move on Ian's part. He brought him from the firehouse where he had kept him for Herb since last winter's persistent frigid weather.

A special cat brush and an igloo-shaped cat habitat were part of the package he brought home. They helped control Snowball's endless white hairs sticking to furniture, carpets, and bed linens—a major reason the Meadow's pet had ended up at the fire station in the first place.

Helsi assigned cat-brushing duty to everyone on a rotating basis and tried to be tolerant when her black or navy wool pants were not fit to be worn out of the house.

Snowball brought great comfort to Mercedes, and she was diligent about feeding him and letting him out to do his business. The other children offered to take turns, but she was adamant about doing it herself every time.

Helsi understood Mercedes' need as a guest not to cause any trouble and to keep Snowball close. But she could not figure out why the child refused to play. On visits, she had enjoyed board games, pretending with dolls and the dollhouse, even shooting baskets outside with the boys.

Her father had called her on the webcam three times since his departure a week ago. They emailed regularly.

She received a letter from Phyllis soon after she arrived at the Bradford's. Helsi wanted to read it but, of course, she could not.

Teachers and Dr. Fleming reported that she was fully engaged at school though somewhat quieter than she had been before.

Not to worry, Helsi told herself. She just needs time to adjust.

Helsi turned her thoughts to work. She had landed the cleaning contract for Dr. Joe Grover at River Edge Pain Clinic. Her new hire, Vinny Stroh, a psychology major at City University, seemed like a workhorse who was anxious to do a good job. He needed the money.

She wanted to prepare him herself so arranged to meet him at the Wednesday-night job for hands-on training.

Robbie arrived home hungry as a bear and complaining about Mr. Maynor.

"Just eat an orange to tide you over, son," she said, pouring hot pudding into dessert cups. She handed him the pan and spoon to lick and began to peel an orange.

Robbie licked the pan and spoon clean and put them in the sink. He took the orange from his mother and finished peeling it.

"Where are those girls?" he asked, blushing slightly.

"They have their Brownie meeting today, Robbie? Did you see them at lunch? They were wearing their badge sashes?"

"I was too upset to notice anything at lunch," he said. "Mom, you need to turn Mr. Maynor in to Dr. Fleming. He doesn't get it."

"What is he guilty of doing?" Helsi asked, setting the table. Robbie stepped close to her, grimacing. "He said he was going to stop letting Conflict Managers be cafeteria helpers. Do you believe that, Mom?" Robbie backed slowly around the table to get out of her way.

"Why is that a problem?" she asked.

"Why is that a problem? Robbie was right under her nose. "The problem is now everyone wants to quit CM or lunchroom duty—or maybe both."

"Everyone?"

"Well, almost everyone."

"I'm sure Dr. Fleming will take care of it, Robbie," Helsi said. "Go relax and eat your orange now."

She was impatient to get on with her chores before time to meet Vinny. And her mind was on coaching points she dare not forget.

She thought of nothing else until time to leave for work and drilled herself in the car on the way.

~ ~ ~

Ian met Helsi at the door. "I'm glad you're home, Hon," he said a bit desperately.

"Why is that, Ian?" she asked, giving him a quick hug. "Mercedes isn't feeling well," he said, following her as she hung up her coat, washed her hands, and rinsed empty popcorn bowls in the sink.

"What do you think is wrong?" she asked, pouring herself a cup of coffee. She raised her eyebrows at Ian and nodded toward the coffeepot.

"No thanks, I just finished a cup," he said. "I can't put my finger on it. She has no fever. Her blood-oxygen level is normal, reflexes normal, eyes clear. She tests out as okay." He shrugged.

"What complaint does she have?" Helsi asked, willing herself to stop mentally reviewing details she had covered with Vinny and focus on Ian's explanation.

"Nothing that points to anything. Just dry throat, stomach ache, headache. She was fine during dinner." Ian took out his medical kit and began to organize it.

"When did it—how did Mercedes bring it to your attention?" Helsi asked, anxiety rising in her chest. She emptied her briefcase and pulled out pages of notes on coaching Vinny.

"She didn't. Lucy did. She brought the child to me fresh from her bath and asked that I check her, said she seemed tired and quiet in the tub."

"What happened between dinner and baths?" Helsi asked, furrowing her brow.

"She played Scrabble with the kids. Then Herb called on the webcam, and she talked to him about twenty minutes—wait a minute!" Ian interrupted himself.

"What?" Helsi asked.

"I tried to give her privacy, Hon. I left the room," Ian said. "But I couldn't help hearing her ask her father if she could go to Belgium and live with him."

"He must have told her no because she grew more intense, begging him. I heard her shout, 'I'm sick, Daddy. I'm getting sick again! I need you.' "

They turned anxious faces toward one another but said nothing, leaving unspoken thoughts hanging in the air.

Chapter Twenty-Two
Hope

"But Bernard," Hope insisted. "You must go to the safety deposit box and find that green envelope."

"Refresh my memory, Hope. Why is the green envelope so important again?" Bernard said in a tired voice.

"We won't know if it's important until we see Item #247, Bernard," she said, feeling a bit put off by his apathy. He's the attorney; he should be interested in every avenue related to this case. He should be initiating the search for this green envelope, she thought.

"Oh very well," he said. "We'll get an intern to go over there and ferret it out. I must hang up now, Dr. Fleming."

"An intern?" Hope was horrified. "But Item #247 might be incriminating to me," she asserted. "You cannot have some intern with a cavalier attitude retrieving the document. Why, it could end up the main topic in the happy-hour discussion at Lola's Bar." She breathed deeply.

"You forget that I am a public servant, Bernard. Scandalous publicity could ruin me," she continued.

"I see then. You are right, Hope," he said, suddenly alert. "I'll do it myself. I'll do it today. But don't count on that paper. Goodbye."

The dial tone buzzed in her ear.

The office door opened slightly and Corinne peeked around it.

"Dr. Fleming," she whispered, stepping inside and closing the door softly behind her.

Hope saw apprehension behind her serene face.

"What is it, Corinne?" she asked.

"Felice Taylor is here; she wants to see you." She glanced toward the door. "I don't know, Hope. I'm afraid to let her in here. I just do not trust her."

"How does she seem? Is she calm?" Hope asked.

"Oh, she's calm all right. But she has a large bag on her arm."

"And?" Hope asked.

"What if she's—what if she's armed?" Corinne asked.

"What does she want? Perhaps you should get the police here before I see her," Hope said, uncharacteristically fearful.

"They're on their way. They'll park in the back and come in the boiler-room door. They're going to text me when they are in the back supply room." Corinne took a breath and held up her cell phone.

Who is still in the building, Hope wondered. Latchkey children were still here, but they were having a jump-rope class in the upstairs gymnasium. She asked Corinne to text the caretaker to keep all children upstairs until notified, the coordinator to send arriving parents upstairs.

"Corinne, have all the teachers gone home?" she whispered.

"All but Bluewave, Hope. You know how she stays until the last dog dies," Corinne said.

The sound of wooden-soled sandals interrupted them.

"Here she comes now," they said in unison. They heard her walk to her mailbox where she turned her tag to read OUT.

They heard her call a warm greeting to Felice and looked uneasily at one another. Both rushed to the door into the outer office.

"Goodnight, Mrs. Stonecipher," Corinne said, looking sideways at Felice, who sat small and tight on a chair, hugging a large tote bag.

Hope called goodnight to Bluewave, and both women watched her leave the building.

"Mrs. Taylor," Hope said. "How are you managing?"

"I need to speak to you," Felice said forcefully and rose.

"I'll be with you in just a moment, Mrs. Taylor. I'm waiting for a call back from a worried mother whose child did not get off the bus." She avoided looking at Felice's dark face. "It should not take long."

"Would you like a coffee, Mrs. Taylor?" Corinne asked, punching keys on her phone.

"I'm fine," she said curtly. "I just need to see the principal."

Hope looked squarely at Felice. No longer willing to be intimidated by this woman, she said, "You may as well come into my office." She held the door open and gestured to her to enter.

Felice walked tall, her body language screaming defiance. Behind her back, Corinne waved her cell phone at Hope and pointed toward the back room. She mouthed the words: Here ! Now!

Hope left the door ajar and invited Felice to sit down. She looked pointedly at the door for a few seconds then met Hope's eyes.

"You and I both know you're the one who delivered the final blow to Chuck and my marriage," she began in an even voice.

Hope felt fear rising in her stomach. She swallowed but did not break eye contact with her visitor.

"You'd better not deny it either," Felice continued, keeping her eyes on Hope while digging in her tote bag.

From the outer office, the sound of two sets of footsteps and jangling keys interrupted her verbal attack.

"Hello Officer Clayton," Corinne said more loudly than necessary. She looked at his partner. "I don't believe I've met you."

The principal and the angry, estranged wife listened as Officer Clayton introduced Officer Powell to the secretary. They heard the ensuing small talk, and Hope felt great relief though a resolute Felice still dug in her bag. Her insolent mood did not break.

Rising briskly with a quick "Excuse me please" and opening wide the door, Hope called to the officers. "How are you, Officer Clayton, Officer Powell?" she asked, stepping forward to shake both their hands.

The officers walked toward her, backing her into her office.

"Hello," they said nonchalantly to Felice.

"Dr. Fleming," Officer Clayton said, smiling. "There's a car parked in the fire lane outside." He turned abruptly toward Felice.

"Oh. Could that be your vehicle?" he asked.

The officers ended up taking her outside, running a check on her, and searching her bag where they found a thick wedding album—and a loaded revolver.

She explained that she carried the gun for protection because of all the lies Chuck had spread about her injuring him. People were leaving telephone and email hate messages "as if she were some kind of evil pervert."

She insisted she had no intention of harming Dr. Fleming. She simply wanted to ask her to take their wedding album to Chuck since there was a restraining order filed, barring her from any contact with him.

"He paid for it," she said. "And it was his idea to order the biggest and the best. Now it's a meaningless piece of trash."

In the end, they took Felice Taylor to the station with them, promising to let Hope and Corinne know the charges that would be filed.

She's already facing Chuck's charge of attempted murder although I don't think she's been indicted yet. How could she be so foolish as to carry a gun—into a school yet, Hope wondered.

"I picked up a message from the parent line, Hope," Corinne said, handing her a note. "It was Mrs. Bradford calling to say Mercedes Meadow would be absent tomorrow and perhaps the next day, too."

They exchanged puzzled looks and said goodnight as Corinne left for the day.

~ ~ ~

After all Latchkey children had been collected by their parents and everyone except night custodian Rosie had gone home, Hope put on her jacket and gathered her things, switching off her desk lamp. The kitschy wedding album stared up from its place on the round table. Its silvery engraving glowed in the dark, mocking her.

An exhausted Hope arrived at the Canterbury Road house completely spent, ready to kiss the ground of her sanctuary. She had planned to review her notes for the fourth-grade faculty meeting on explicit phonics but was too emotionally drained to concentrate.

She changed into flannel lounge pants and a cardigan, brewed a cup of tea, and made a tomato cheese sandwich. Still hungry, she ate two large dark-chocolate, oatmeal cookies. Looking down at the clothes she wore and the cookie in her hand, she thought, who is this person in my skin?

When Bernard rang to say he had located item#247, Hope feared it would be a ledger page—or pages. She waited without breathing for him to explain.

"Well Hope, as it turns out, item #247 is important. It's very important." He inhaled then exhaled loudly. "It concerns you. In fact, it should mitigate Franklin Baldwin's case considerably."

"What sort of document is it, Bernard?" Hope asked, afraid to know.

"It's a codicil."

"A codicil? What is that? How is it spelled?"

"It's spelled c-o-d-i-c-i-l. It is an amendment to a will, in this case, to Mary Baldwin's will."

Hope's heart raced. "What does it say?"

"You'll be utterly surprised, Hope. Come into the office tomorrow morning before eight."

She explained that she had a faculty meeting at seven thirty and would try to come later in the morning.

"Not possible, I'm afraid. I'll be on a ten fifteen plane to Washington."

"So you are off to see your Andover schoolmate, now our esteemed Education Secretary?"

"That's right." He cleared his throat. "Do you have a message for William?"

"I certainly do, Bernard, regarding all his fuss about merit pay."

"Of course, merit pay, a splendid idea, don't you think?" he chided.

She swallowed and began, "Please tell your Mr. Wertheimer that he has managed to unsettle many teachers—good teachers. They worry about special-needs students, those with no home support, poor test takers, transient families. They want to know if teachers will have a voice in the way class groupings are formed. You know teachers, by nature, plan ahead. They make sure all the bases are covered for their kids." She rubbed her temples.

"Please tell William Wertheimer," she continued, "that he must not go around tossing out complex issues like merit pay with no explanation, no criteria, no thought-out policy," She sighed.

"I will mention merit pay, Hope, if I find the right moment for such a contentious issue," he said dryly.

"If I must wait to see the codicil, please just tell me what it says," Hope said, not liking his matter-of-fact response to her request.

"You will be speechless; I was," Bernard said. "You will hear from me Sunday. Goodbye, Hope."

~ ~ ~

Fourth-grade teachers were at frustration level. After reviewing literature on explicit phonics and discussing it to the –nth degree, everyone seemed confused.

"I don't get it, Desiree Osmond said with furrowed brow. "I know that first-grade teachers spend a lot of time on beginning letter sounds and breaking words into syllables. So our kids have had explicit phonics, have they not?"

Reading specialist, Debbie Maher, said, "I know, Desiree. But they also expose early readers to whole words along with beginning letter sounds." She looked around the room for a supportive face. "They don't really push word attack, syllable-by-syllable the way the explicit-phonics people seem to be recommending. 'Explicit phonics moves from the smallest parts to the whole,' according to them. That's where we fall short. Isn't that right, Dr. Fleming?" She turned from Desiree toward Hope.

Tension hung thickly in the room.

"Do you know how tedious it is to drill and drill a child on letter sounds, syllable-by-syllable every reading period, every day?" Brad Kushner said. "I taught first grade. The kids—the average and above, that is—thought it was all a no-brainer. They were hungry for whole words."

"Brad makes a good point," Debbie Maher said. "The average and above students may not seem to need explicit phonics in the primary grades. They know their letter sounds; they know how to syllabize." She looked around the room and rested her gaze on Hope. "They do fine with the readers and workbooks for their grade level."

"I see what you're saying, Debbie," Sam Pavlik added. "But when they come to us in fourth grade, and they don't have that controlled vocabulary in their social studies and science books; they get into trouble. They can't syllabize." He smiled at everyone. "How'd I do with Debbie's five-dollar, reading-specialist word?"

Everyone laughed and Hope was grateful for the comic relief.

She had to provide a clear summary of what needed to be done to help teachers of fourth-graders improve their word-attack skills for reading in other subjects.

"You have made many good points:

- Brad brought out the idea that average- and above-readers do well with our program as it is.

- Debbie reminded us that below-average readers need to learn mastery on word attack and syllabizing to stay on grade level.

- Sam concluded that all fourth graders need a strong word-attack foundation for understanding unfamiliar words in their content-area reading."

"In grade four, the emphasis shifts from learning to read to reading to learn. Without the ability to break down unfamiliar words in the content areas like science and social studies, their reading is weak. If an unfamiliar word cannot be heard by the ear—sounded out—comprehension will not happen."

Hope closed with a promise to bring in an expert for a reading workshop for all faculty.

"Our mystery contestant for the spring talent show has confirmed. S/he will be a big hit with you AND the children," she announced, before adjourning the meeting.

Teachers fell to laughing and joking about the talent show and past mystery contestants as they filed out just before first bell.

That was a good discussion, Hope deduced, gathering folders and papers.

Item #247 filled her mind as she hurried down the hall. I'll have no peace until Sunday, she thought. Bernard McElson is a cruel man.

Chapter Twenty-Three

Ray

Fiona sipped strong coffee at their kitchen table with young Josh Wentworth and his father Wes. Josh avoided all eye contact, his eyes studying the oak tabletop intensely. Wes, however, seemed relaxed and pleasant.

"Thank you, Mr. Wentworth and Josh, for agreeing to see me today. As you can imagine, your input is important to my client's case."

"I understand," Wes said, offering more coffee.

Josh's history of false testimony hung palpably in the air.

"No, no, I'm fine," Fiona said, smiling. "But I will have a little more milk, if you please."

Wes fetched a creamer and sat back down.

"Okay. What can we do for you, Ms. Fitzenrider?" he asked.

"I really need to ask Josh a few questions about the night Mr. Sellers drove him and the other boys home after finding them out along the highway in the dark." She looked at Josh with kind eyes, waiting for him to turn to her.

"Josh," Wes said, nudging the boy's knee. "Son, pay attention to Ms. Fitzenrider. She needs your help. It's very important." He lifted Josh's chin.

Fiona felt the tension between them.

"That's better, Josh," Fiona said. "Now Josh, I need you to listen carefully to the questions and try very hard to remember exactly what happened that night."

Josh kept his eyes on her without wavering.

"And it's necessary that you be as truthful as you can possibly be, she said, locking her eyes with his. "If you have ever told a fib or a white lie before, this is not the time to do that. You must stand up with the truth. You must do the right thing."

"Josh," she said, turning her shoulders toward him. "I understand that you and Tommy Grant are best friends. Is that right?"

The boy squirmed in his seat and looked into space. "We're just friends," he said, dropping his voice and avoiding her eyes.

"Best friends?" she asked.

"No, just friends—not best." He avoided her eyes. "I haven't known him very long," he said to the walls. "He's on my baseball team."

"So you don't feel you know Tommy that well, Josh?"

"Not that well," he muttered, dropping his chin again.

"Josh, I know that Mr. Sellers found you, Tommy, and little Andrew out along the highway after dark. Is that correct?"

"Yes," he murmured.

"Yes, that is correct?" Fiona asked.

"Sit up, Son," Wes instructed.

"Yes, that is correct," he said.

"Yes, that is correct, Ms. Fitzenrider," Wes prompted.

"Yes, that is correct, Ms. Fitzenrider," Josh said, sitting up straighter and meeting her eyes.

"So when Mr. Sellers wanted to get you home safely, Tommy, little Andrew, and you climbed into the backseat and away you went." She smiled. "Is that right, Josh?"

"That's … right," he said, falteringly. He swallowed and blushed. "But then Mr. Sellers told Tommy to ride in the front." He looked past Fiona.

"Did he give a reason Tommy should ride in the front, Josh?"

"No, he just said, 'Get in the front.' " He did not look at her. Fiona thought of the coach, the step-grandfather, unjustly accused by Josh.

She questioned the boy at length about the weather that night, what the boys were doing out along the highway, who was dropped off first, and whether the seating order changed at any point.

"When we dropped off the kid—Andy, Tommy jumped out so the kid wouldn't have to climb over his huge feet. Mr. Sellers made a big deal out of how polite Tommy was. I didn't think it was such a big thing. But even Andy's mother was impressed. She called Tommy a good role model. The rest of the time she scowled at everyone, even Mr. Sellers." He stopped to take a breath.

Fiona and Wes looked at each other knowingly.

"So Tommy started out in the backseat and stayed there the entire ride home. Is that what you remember, Josh?" Fiona asked.

"I guess so," he said, becoming surly.

"You don't guess, Josh. You have to tell the truth as you remember it," his father said, an edge to his voice. "Now tell Ms. Fitzenrider the facts. Tommy either sat in the back seat or he did not. Which was it?"

Fiona felt the intimidating tone of his voice and turned to see his threatening eyes. Obviously Josh had seen this side of Wes before.

"Tommy sat in the back seat until we got to his house," Josh said.

"And that's the truth?" she asked.

"And that's the truth," he said.

"And you'll tell the truth to the judge," Wes said.

On the drive back to her office, Fiona pored over Josh's responses. It was difficult to tell whether his own contradictory stories tripped him up or he was so intimidated by his father that he decided to tell the real truth. Perhaps he had learned from his past sins.

~ ~ ~

Mrs. Billings was a different sort. She claimed not to remember where the boys sat in Ray's car and smoke-screened with a litany of complaints against Poore Pond School, Dr. Fleming, and Ray Sellers. It was obvious that she had no desire to help any of them.

But after Fiona brought up the fact that her six-year-old son was out along the highway after dark with two older boys and how that could amount to child neglect—even child endangering, Mrs. Billings' recall faculties returned.

She clearly remembered the scenario with all three boys in the backseat and Tommy's stepping out so Andrew did not have to climb over him. Her account matched Josh's. She remembered seeing Josh, whom she described accurately, sitting in the back as well.

Furthermore, she agreed to testify to those facts.

~ ~ ~

Ray was frying hamburgers and a veggie burger for Heather when Fiona called. She gave a short summary of her meetings with Josh and his father and with Mrs. Billings.

"So far so good, Ray," she said optimistically. "Tomorrow I have an informal meeting with Mr. Grant."

"Well, I really hope that turns out as well as your meetings today, Fiona," Ray said, cradling the phone in his shoulder and turning the burgers in the skillet.

"Please tell Heather not to worry, that things are going your way; and we will definitely be ready for May twenty-fourth."

"I'll tell her that," Ray said. "Thanks, Fiona."

"Good-bye, Ray. I'll call you after I see Dick Grant."

He replaced the phone and slid the burgers onto buns, laying the platter next to the tray Heather had prepared with rows of lettuce, tomato, and onion.

"Heather! Jeremy! Dinner's ready," he called. Heather came in wearing a terrycloth robe with a towel around her hair. Jeremy followed, carrying an action figure.

"You were in the shower, Hon. I thought you were resting," he said. He handed her the veggie burger on a plate.

"I did rest awhile," she said. "I shampooed my hair tonight, so I would have more time in the morning. Jeremy starts achievement testing tomorrow, and I want to make sure he has a proper breakfast." She sat down across from her son.

"Apple pancakes, Ray," he said, smiling. "That's what I'm having. And Mom found cinnamon syrup."

"I could give him a proper breakfast, Heather; I'm home," Ray said softly, a trace of dejection in his voice.

"Don't you have an early appointment with Fiona, Ray?" she asked.

"No. She just called, said everything went our way today with the witnesses she questioned. She said to tell you that and that we will be ready by the trial date." His eyes searched her face for a reaction as he pulled out a chair and sat at the table.

Heather reached across and put her hand on his. "That's good to hear."

"Will I go to court with you, Mom?" Jeremy asked.

"I don't think so, Jeremy," she said softly.

"Maybe Ray wants me there," he said looking at Ray.

"It would cheer me up to have you there, Jeremy," Ray said. "But it might be upsetting for you. Trials are dirty business."

"Ooohh," he whined then took a big bite of burger.

"We'll be getting a new manager in the pharmacy around the time of your trial date, Ray," Heather said softly. "She came in and introduced herself today."

Ray did not like hearing that. "That's not good timing, is it, Hon?" He smiled tenderly at her. "Is she a nice kind of woman?"

"Seems to be, she said," pushing her plate away with an uneaten half veggie burger on it. "Don't you worry about me, Ray; you have enough to think about, getting your case ready with Fiona and all." She rose and carried plates to the sink, patting his shoulder as she passed.

"Mom, may I stay up an extra half hour tonight?" Jeremy asked, assuming a pathetic look on his angelic face. "I haven't had time with you and Ray for a week."

Ray looked at Heather, not wanting to see her refuse the boy.

He really needs more time with us, he thought.

Heather hesitated, her lips poised to say no. She looked at her husband's sympathetic expression and paused.

"Just half an hour, Jeremy. You want to be in good shape for your big test tomorrow," she said, enjoying his smile and Ray's.

They played Uno for three, acting silly and laughing like babies, eating buttery popcorn Ray had made.

"I'm tired, Ray," Heather said after tucking in Jeremy. "I'm going to bed now, too."

"I'll join you," he said, suddenly feeling worn out. "Do you mind if I watch a little TV in bed?"

They snuggled in front of the television watching an old movie Ray found. Heather fell asleep in minutes.

Ray tried to get his mind off Tommy Grant and his father but kept remembering the awkward meeting they'd had when he drove Tommy home and waited for the man. There was something edgy about him, a sort of evasiveness. He was distant and cold and had not thanked Ray for waiting or for driving his son home.

At the time, Ray sensed Grant knew that he and his wife should not have left the boy on his own that night. That obvious fact hung in the air along with unspoken words of concern for his son.

Ray recalled having seen Grant at school a few times and saying hello to him in passing, noting his unnatural manner. He always seemed guarded, tense—like a man with something to hide. Well, if that's the case, he thought, Fiona will ferret it out for sure. He pressed the off button on the remote and turned on his side to snuggle in the quilts.

~ ~ ~

Fiona balanced a large pizza box, bag of chocolate donuts, and a briefcase as she rang the doorbell at the Grant house. She could not see her wristwatch but knew that she was half an hour early.

Tommy opened the door and immediately called out to his father.

"We weren't expecting you yet," Mr. Grant said, not opening the storm door.

"I'm a little early, but I've brought dinner," she said, undaunted. "May I come in?" She smiled warmly.

He opened the door reluctantly; and she stepped inside, handing him the box.

"I'm Fiona Fitzenrider, in case you don't remember, Mr. Grant."

"Hi Tommy," she said to the boy lurking in the background. "Do you like pizza?" She handed him the donuts.

"Where shall we talk?" she asked, looking for a clue to how the rooms were used since every space was in disarray.

"We'll go in the kitchen," he said, leading the way around the clutter of newspapers, boxes, jackets, and the like.

"I'll just follow you, Mr. Grant," she laughed.

"Call me Dick," he said to her over his shoulder. "Tommy, you go downstairs and occupy yourself.

Mrs. Fitzenrider and I have to talk."

"Take the pizza, Tommy," she said, "And a donut."

Dick led her to the table. She waited while he removed condiments and crumbs from the tabletop then gestured for her to sit down.

"Thank you, Mr. Grant—Dick, for agreeing to speak with me off the record," she said, smiling.

"No problem," he said, looking through the window. "Anything I can do to help get at the truth, I'm glad to do." He cleared his throat.

"I admire your thinking," she said. "My client deserves the truth. His reputation, his very livelihood are at stake here." Her eyes sought his, but he looked past her.

She pulled papers from her briefcase and settled herself in a chair.

"Excuse me," he said and stepped out. She overheard him in the hallway instructing his son to take his pizza and drink downstairs and not to come up until called.

"We have grownup talk to get through, and you don't need

to hear it."

That's a surefire way to make the boy sneak up and eavesdrop, she thought, secretly delighted that the little scalawag was likely going to follow her plan.

Dick Grant returned and offered her coffee. They made small talk while he prepared cups for both of them. She insisted he enjoy pizza as they talked informally.

Fiona reviewed the points in Tommy's testimony and the non-points in Dick's bland statements.

"I found Mr. Sellers in my kitchen when I arrived home that night. He seemed to be in a hurry to leave," Fiona read aloud from Dick's statement. Her eyes met his but she was unable to read him.

'Dick, Tommy accused Mr. Sellers of molesting him more than a year ago, when he was still a student at Poore Pond School," she said dully.

"That's right, out behind the dumpster. I've seen that dumpster. It's gigantic," he said, still expressionless though making a point.

"Did your son report these allegations to you at the time—or at anytime, for that matter? Or to his mother? Surely she would have told you if he had, would she not?" Fiona watched his face, waiting for him to lift his eyes.

"No, he did not, never told me about any of them." He looked squarely at her. "His mother never mentioned it either; and yes, she would have told me if she knew."

She asked about the history of his marriage, Tommy's age when the divorce took place, the boy's relationships with his biological mother and his stepmother.

She asked about custody arrangements.

"I understand that you and Tommy's mother have shared custody. Is that right?"

"Well, …technically we do," Dick said, looking into space. "But."

Fiona waited.

"But his mother doesn't really do her part. She dumps the boy on me most of the time."

Fiona asked leading questions about that point and was certain he was not being forthright. She had spoken to the first Mrs. Grant, who had given her evidence that Dick was the one not doing his part in the shared custody arrangement.

In fact, this was Tommy's week to be at his mother's house, but his father had insisted on taking him today to "pitch balls and work on his batting for baseball season."

"Were you not in favor of a shared custody agreement, Dick?" she asked.

"No, I wasn't," he said, meeting her gaze. "It's not fair to the kid, shuttling back and forth every week like that."

"What agreement would you have preferred?" she asked.

"Full custody with visitation for the noncustodial parent," he said readily.

"So you wanted full custody of Tommy. Is that right?" she asked although she had read the entire transcript of the custody proceedings.

"Well—yes, I did," he said uncertainly.

"But you did not formally request that, did you, Dick? Why not?" She studied his body language carefully.

"I didn't know what I wanted at the time." He hung his head. "I was so devastated by the divorce—I was confused."

"You wanted your wife to be the custodial parent, so you would have less responsibility for the boy. Is that right?"

"No that's not right," he said, his voice firm. "That's not right at all." He gulped coffee.

"Mr. Grant, I'm not trying to upset you." Fiona began. "But I've read all the court transcripts, and I've spoken to your ex-wife. The fact is you were not even sure you wanted to be a father. And your lack of interest in the boy was a major factor in the divorce, was it not?"

"I don't care what's in the record," he said, redness moving up his neck. "I love my son. Of course I want to be his father. I just don't know how to do it. My father was absent without leave. He abandoned us. I never learned what it means to be a father." He covered his face with his hands.

"That's unfortunate, Mr. Grant. But the fact is you asked for shared custody to avoid paying full child support. The stipulation was that you attend parenting classes in order to become the father you professed in court you wanted to be."

Dick stood and looked at her with utter loathing.

"You also made accusations about your wife's alleged promiscuity and drug use to keep her from getting full custody." Fiona said, rising.

"You manipulated the court into a shared-custody agreement by casting doubt on your wife's character and pleading your own deprived childhood as the cause of your irresponsibility to the child," Fiona continued relentlessly.

"Leave this house now!" Dick shouted.

"You were so convincing that you managed to get a requirement that your wife have supervision during her initial weeks of shared custody. She had to have her sister or mother stay with her when Tommy was there," Fiona fired away.

"You leave or I'm calling the police," Dick demanded, brandishing a cell phone.

Fiona hurried to the door. "You'll hear from the court," she called over her shoulder. Letting herself out, she glanced toward the small face watching from the shadows of the hallway.

Chapter Twenty-Four
The Bradfords

Helsi sat at a table with the principal, Mercedes' teacher, the school psychologist, and the nurse. On the table lay an array of clinic slips representing each visit the child had made to the clinic in one week's time.

"We're glad you called with your concerns, Mrs. Bradford." Dr. Fleming said. "Daily visits to the clinic went on all last week and sent up a big red flag. But we wanted to give the child a little more time before raising an alarm."

"You sent a good report the first week Mercedes came to live with us," Helsi commented. "Since then has there been a change in her attitude toward her work, in her performance, or anything else? Other than her quietness, I mean."

"Not much of a change," Lou Ann Newhouse said. "She's still mostly silent in class. We were encouraged when she signed up for the end-of-school assembly, remembering what a good master of ceremonies she'd been last year."

"But she didn't get to be in the actual assembly, did she?" psychologist Carol Davis recalled. "She was absent."

"And she wrote the class skit; it was wonderfully done," Mrs. Newhouse said.

"Yes, and her performance at dress rehearsal was outstanding as well," Mrs. Davis said.

"Will she be master of ceremonies again?" Helsi asked. "She's in this quiet phase; I can't see her announcing if she doesn't get back to herself."

"These regular visits to the clinic," Nurse Sunfield said, waving the forms in her hand, "indicate that she's nowhere near getting back to herself. She confides in me that she is moving to Belgium to live with her father."

"Nurse Sunfield, what happens in the clinic?" Helsi asked, looking at her with sad eyes.

"Oh, the standard procedure," Nurse said. "I know she needs a little TLC, but we do take her temperature." She scrubbed her hands. "I try to drag it out, chitchat to show interest in her, have her drink water, take her pulse, ask what her symptoms are, that sort of thing."

Helsi listened intently, trying to drive away her fears. Thank God her temps were normal, according to those slips, she thought.

In the end, the team outlined a plan to give Mercedes a sounding board through meetings with the psychologist three times a week.

Dr. Fleming cautioned her to be especially watchful for symptoms that the child might be developing Munchausen Syndrome herself.

Helsi remembered Mercedes' plea of sickness to her father on the webcam call and was grateful for Hope's reminder to Mrs. Davis.

That evening after dinner and children's bedtime, Helsi filled Ian in on the meeting at school.

"What did Dr. Fleming mean by saying 'Mercedes might be developing Munchausen Syndrome herself'?" he asked. "I thought Phyllis was the one with the disease, intentionally making her child sick."

Helsi went to her desk and brought back a printout of the Cleveland Clinic report on Munchausen Syndrome by Proxy, which included mention of Munchausen Syndrome. She handed it to Ian. He read aloud from Helsi's highlighted paragraph in the report:

> *In some cases, a child victim of MSP learns
> to associate getting attention to being sick and
> develops Munchausen syndrome him or herself.[12]*

Their somber eyes met. Neither spoke.

"I think we'd better call Herb," Ian said finally.

They discussed the worst-possible progression of Mercedes' symptoms and felt overwhelmed.

They found themselves scouring cupboards for any and all medications, both prescription and over-the-counter. They put them all in a lockbox which they stored high on a shelf in their closet. They each took one of the two keys in the lock and clipped it to their keychains.

They made plans to take the family to the circus on the weekend, hoping to bring Mercedes out of herself.

Nobody was more excited than Rachel. She had been troubled and confused by Mercedes' reticence and unwillingness to play. She managed to get the girl to help create a circus mural with drawings and magazine cutouts.

Helsi broke her own rule and let them use her brown glue since there was no children's white glue in the bottle. Mercedes even made a paper crown for Snowball, King of the Circus. They taped the mural to the hallway wall, and the entire family admired it.

For that brief time, the child was engaged again, much like the old days. But once the mural was hung, she reverted to her protective shell.

At dinner, she suddenly announced she felt sick and rushed to the bathroom, upchucking ferociously in the toilet. Helsi sat on the floor, rubbing her back until she finished. She washed her thoroughly.

Ian checked her carefully and sent for the ambulance. Emergency-room doctors determined that the child had ingested some sort of foreign substance. Tests and examination by a specialist revealed she had taken a substance containing chemicals found in certain adhesives.

They traced the chemical to Helsi's brown glue, and she was beside herself. The brown glue went up on the closet shelf into the lockbox.

Ian tried several times to call Herb on the web.

The night of the circus, Mercedes again upchucked violently. Lucy found a paper cup with drops of pink shampoo in the bottom. Ian scrutinized the bottle and called the poison center.

At Helsi's urging, Ian took the family to the circus without Mercedes and her. She spent the time holding the child, who was holding Snowball, on her lap while they read circus and animal stories. The girl seemed happy and smiling and even took turns reading.

She tucked the sleepy child into bed before the others arrived home and went downstairs.

Sipping herbal tea to calm her anxiety, she pondered Mercedes' situation. It seemed so simple. The child just needed her mother. She tried to think of ways to spend more time alone with her then felt guilty that she wasn't doing that for Rachel, her youngest.

She chastised herself for reinforcing Mercedes' manipulative ways of getting attention by making the attention complete and so pleasurable.

She tried to call Herb on the web, realizing too late the time change and that his workday was just beginning. There was no answer of course.

When they finally reached Herb and gave him a rundown of his daughter's bouts of illness and her state of withdrawal, he suggested they take her to see Phyllis.

"There was always a strong bond between them," he said. "Her mother seems to be able to calm her down."

His remarks stunned Ian and Helsi. It was as if he had forgotten why his wife was incarcerated.

~ ~ ~

Against their better judgment, they traveled with Mercedes to the State Hospital for the Criminally Insane. She seemed excited about seeing her mother again, chatting a bit on the long drive.

"Mercedes dearest," Phyllis said when they walked into the visitation room. "Come here, darling." She hugged her daughter tightly and the child hugged back, hanging onto her desperately for what seemed like minutes.

Phyllis invited Ian and Helsi to sit down. She lifted her daughter onto her lap.

The girl kept staring at Phyllis' hair, now more grey than blonde and swept into a sleek bun in back. She gave her clothes a once-over, too. The shapeless, faded-green cotton wrap dress was unlike anything she had ever seen her mother wear.

"Mommy," she said finally. "Why are you dressed like that? Why is your hair so funny?"

Phyllis looked at her with hostile eyes and lifted her onto the floor in one harsh movement. She stood, touching her hand to her forehead.

"Please take her away now. It's obvious she hasn't a care for her mother."

Mercedes hugged her legs frantically, "No, Mommy. I love you. I want to stay with you!"

An attendant appeared and escorted Phyllis away, leaving a sobbing daughter who had to be restrained from running after her.

~ ~ ~

Helsi sat in the backseat with her arms around the heartbroken child, stroking her face and singing softly.

It took half an hour or more for Mercedes to relax and fall asleep, her hair damp, skin clammy and red.

Ian pulled into a drive-through restaurant and bought sandwiches and drinks for the three of them. Helsi set Mercedes' food aside for later.

She was bursting to discuss with Ian what had happened at the hospital but did not dare to in the girl's presence, even if she did seem to be asleep. She took large drinks of strong coffee and tried to think about the upcoming work week. We should call Herb, she thought. Mercedes needs a family member.

"We need to call Herb again, Helsi," Ian said from the driver's seat, echoing his wife's thoughts.

After several attempts to reach him by webcam and email, they stopped trying and arranged for Mercedes to see a pediatric psychotherapist.

The child warmed immediately to Dr. Fiske, a kindhearted mother figure who spent hours interviewing Ian, Helsi, and Mercedes separately. She put the child through a battery of personality and psychological as well as laboratory tests.

Dr. Fiske interviewed the Bradford children, both separately and as a group, sometimes including Mercedes, at which time she invited Helsi and Ian to observe from behind a see-through mirror.

Mercedes responded to all the attention by reverting to her characteristic happy and engaged self.

Dr. Fiske shared a poem the girl had written, her impressions of her two-week procedure at the clinic during which she was under the microscope, so to speak.

> I miss Mommy every day.
> It hurts my heart.
> But when I go to Dr. Fiske
> My heart feels better.
>
> She talks to me.
> She listens to me.
> She touches me.
> I feel safe.
>
> The nurses give me medicine and water
> in a glass cup with a glass straw.
> They use instruments to look and listen all
> over my body.
>
> Sometimes Rachel and her family come to
> Dr. Fiske and sit around a table and
> talk. Dr. Fiske calls it a session.
> I feel safe.
>
> Even when the nurses give me pills and
> thick liquid to swallow I feel safe.
> When they stick me with needles I feel safe.
>
> When I grow up I want to be a nurse
> maybe a doctor.
> Daddy will bring Mommy home for
> me to take care of
> And she'll be safe.

"I would like to keep Mercedes confined here as an in-patient until you reach her father, Dr. Fiske said. "It will give me an opportunity for further examination of her deviant conceptual thinking," she said, looking at first Helsi then Ian with questioning eyes.

Their silence was palpable.

It doesn't seem right to farm her out to this clinic until we hear from Herb—God only knows how long that may take, Helsi thought. What would our children think? What would Herb think? And what in the world would Mercedes think? Abandoned first by her mother and then by the only family she knows. But she seems so happy here.

How do I feel about leaving her here, Ian asked himself. It smacks of elective hospitalization, of just dumping the child here because we do not want to care for her. And what about insurance? The entire idea sounds all wrong. But she does seem happy here.

Helsi met Ian's gaze with imploring eyes.

Breaking the silence, Ian turned to the doctor and said, "We'd have to check on the insurance coverage."

Dr. Fiske explained, "It's been my experience that many insurance companies also cover an in-patient period if they cover out-patient treatment for this sort of thing. The financial office can easily check that."

In the end, after insurance coverage was verified for a minimum two-week period—possibly longer in certain cases, the Bradford's agreed to leave Mercedes in the hands of Dr. Fiske for the time being, a matter of a few days only.

~ ~ ~

After trying almost around the clock, they finally reached Herb two days later. At first he was crushed by Dr. Fiske's diagnosis of his beloved daughter: at risk for Munchausen Syndrome; neither was he happy about her confinement at the clinic.

Ian gave him the name of the psychotherapist and her contact numbers, suggesting he might speak to both Dr. Fiske and Mercedes on the same call.

He agreed to get back to them within twenty-four hours.

When his wife was diagnosed with Munchausen Syndrome by Proxy, he had not educated himself on the condition. He understood that it was a mental disorder but had no sense of its symptoms, possible causes, complications, or treatment.

Had he researched for himself—or just read the literature from Phyllis' doctors, he would know that Mercedes, a victim of her mentally ill mother's behavior as an MSP patient, might learn to associate getting attention with being sick. He would know of the possibility that his daughter could develop Munchausen Syndrome and begin to seek attention through her own professed illness.

Herb was as good as his word, calling them back on the webcam the next evening. Apparently after hearing the Bradford's latest report, he'd managed a crash course in Munchausen Syndrome by Proxy and Munchausen Syndrome. And he had undertaken a survey of psychotherapeutic services near Brussels and concluded that "Belgian doctors and hospitals have more advanced treatment than American facilities."

He would arrive in three days and take his daughter back to Belgium where "a team of specialists in a first-rate clinic awaited her."

The entire Bradford family felt defeated. They wanted the best for Mercedes and felt they had given their all.

"We have to put our own children first, Helsi," Ian said. "They don't need to feel responsible for Mercedes' problems." He clicked off the webcam page and turned toward his wife.

"That's right, Hon," Helsi agreed. "They each went out of their way to make Mercedes welcome. They can be proud of that."

"Remember the poem Mercedes wrote, Helsi? The one Dr. Fiske showed us?" Ian asked.

"Remember it, Ian?" she said and looked at him with troubled eyes. "It has haunted me ever since I first read it."

"Me too," Ian said. "If I understand her poem, a hospital is the only place she feels safe—even happy." He shook his head slowly. "How sick is that?"

"It's awful. And the fact that she hopes to become a nurse one day and care for her mother—at home, where she'll be "safe," Helsi said.

Ian joined her on the sofa where she returned to the task of matching pairs of small socks from the dryer. He began to help her.

"We should think about how much to tell the children of Mercedes' illness," he said.

"Definitely," Helsi agreed. "They do not need specifics."

Both were lost in their own thoughts of how to handle Herb's arrival and his daughter's departure with utmost grace in the eyes of everyone concerned.

Chapter Twenty-Five
Hope

Hope woke to birds chirping in the early dawn. Smiling, she threw back the covers, rushed to the windows, and drew open the curtains. The sky looked clear, promising a good-weather day.

Today is Saturday, she said to herself in the shower. Tomorrow is the day Bernard will let me know what Mary wrote in Item#247. Delight engulfed her. Then dread.

She resolved not to make wild guesses about the contents of Item#247, nor to spend time speculating on exactly when she might expect word from Bernard. She knew he had a three-fifteen flight from Washington tomorrow.

She would simply go about her business; he had her cell phone number.

The early morning chill kept her from breakfasting on the terrace, so she made a rare decision to take her tray into the dining room. Through the large front windows, the view of crowded Shasta-daisy beds was perfect.

Separating segments of a juicy navel orange, she reflected on her plans for the day. I will go ahead and meet Theo at the shelter around ten thirty and help him prepare to brief Mark Fleming on the grant-writing assignment he has been hired to do.

I'm happy we were able to give Mark work, she thought, for his sake as well as for George's, who had lobbied long and hard for his uncle. For Michael's sake, too, she surprised herself by feeling. I'm still getting used to the idea of Michael's having a good side.

She tucked heartily into a buttery, six-minute egg and ate an entire rye roll, savoring crunchy crust and tender insides. Even her usual brew of tea tasted exceptional today.

The house phone rang, interrupting pleasant thoughts.

"Good morning," she chirped.

"Good morning, Hope," Bernard said.

"Are you calling from Washington, Bernard?

"Actually, I am calling from your driveway, Hope. Will you please let me in? Do you have coffee?"

"You scamp!" she said and rushed to the door.

She offered him breakfast; he opted for strong coffee and one of her rye rolls with butter and honey.

She brought herself a second cup of tea and settled into the chair at a right angle to him.

Bernard drew a slender, green envelope from his breast pocket and laid it on the table.

Hope's heart quickened. Feeling his eyes fixed on her, she feigned nonchalance and sipped from her teacup. She nibbled at an orange section.

"Did you spend time with your friend, the Education Secretary?" she asked casually. He nodded.

They chatted about Washington and his flight change. "I didn't think it was fair to make you wait until Sunday, Hope," he announced and handed her the green envelope.

"Go ahead, read it, Hope. After you refill my cup."

She took his cup to the coffee brewer and filled it with dark coffee. She willed herself a steady hand as she placed it in front of him.

Opening the flap of the green envelope, she swallowed and removed the folded onionskin paper.

~ ~ ~

Codicil to the will of Mary Margrethe Baldwin
January 22, 1982

I, Mary Margrethe Baldwin, of sound mind and body, freely write this codicil in behalf of my former employee, Hope Minster Fleming.

Hope began work for me in her nineteenth year, advancing from entry-level position of driver, clerical aide, and companion, to that of accountant and private secretary—in a matter of months.

I came to admire greatly, her keen mind, capability for the job, and self–awareness. She knew where she wanted to go and was not afraid of the hard work it would take to get there.

I loved her like a daughter and found immense personal joy in her successes. I gave Hope full authority to write monthly cheques on my account and to cash those written to herself as payee. Let there be no mistake—every last cheque she wrote on my account was written with my full approval.

Hope Minster Fleming has no knowledge of being designated heir to my estate. Any claims made on any portion of this bequest to Hope, by any party, including Frederick Baldwin, shall be deemed invalid.

As testatrix, this is my clear and expressed wish, witnessed by the signees below.

Sincerely and unequivocally,

Mary Margarethe Baldwin

Witnesses:

Elinor Burgeson

Elinor Burgeson
Jan. 22, 1982

Perry Sims

Perry Sims
1/22/82

Hope feared Bernard could hear her still-pounding heart. Sipping tea and savoring it, she stole a sidelong glance at him.

Laying the letter on the table, she willed herself to a calm exterior, hands clasped quietly on her lap, shoulders relaxed, her face a mask of serenity. She licked her lips discreetly and gazed out the front windows.

But her heart and mind were drowning in a montage of emotions.

She read the signatures then sought Bernard's eyes.

He studied her face for emotion, any emotion: surprise, joy, disbelief. He saw nothing.

Hope looked again at the letter and began to reread it slowly, not lifting it. Her eyes filled with tears at Mary's praise and professed love. She looked away.

"Hope, read the last paragraph—the last sentence."

Hope reread the last paragraph and was affronted by the name of her nemesis.

"Frederick……"

"Frederick has no case, Hope," he interrupted. "It does not matter how many audits he demands. Mary Baldwin has given you carte blanche. She apparently knew her step-great grandson quite well."

He stood and brushed crumbs from his lap.

"We will let his attorney play out his research before producing this document. Then it will simply be: case closed."

Bernard left a stunned Hope at the table and saw himself out.

A flurry of emotions swirled in her head: shame, joy, shock, relief, bewilderment. She swallowed to moisten her parched throat and reached for orange juice.

Mary had known all along.

She knew I was stealing and allowed me to do it.

But she loved me. Like a daughter.

Laying her head on the polished table, she wept like a child.

~ ~ ~

Hope could not wait to see Theo. Bright spring sunshine engulfed her as she drove to the shelter. I will not tell Theo about Mary's letter, she told herself. He would have opinions and expect some discussion of the matter. I could not bear his mentioning the word *felony* -not today, not until I come to terms with this enormous gift, this crushing weight that has come down on me.

But she had a gaping need to feel his warmth and the security of his balanced personality, the validation she needed to deal with the *Baldwin Curse,* as she was beginning to think of Item#247.

~ ~ ~

In the end, Mark thanked Hope and Theo repeatedly for the opportunity to write grants that could fund another psychiatrist for shelter clients. He was impressed with the entire operation and especially with the office George arranged for him.

George had told his mother he was having a door cut into the hallway from the small storage room adjoining the kitchen. It sounded very makeshift to her at the time but had turned out well. And he was so adamant about protecting Mark's privacy that only George knew where to find the master key to that door between the kitchen and Uncle Mark's new office.

Theo and Hope reviewed the grant applications with Mark; he was a quick study. With his legal background, he quickly cut through the language and understood the type of information required.

They showed him the files brought from the main office, containing the mission statement, history, and demographics of the shelter as well as the funding and budget.

"Those files are signed out to you, Mark. Keep them in your locked drawer here when you are not working with them." Hope instructed. "You will need to return them to George, Theo, or me when you finish."

"I certainly will, Hope," he said, smiling. "I know all about document safety." He turned toward her. "And thanks again for this opportunity. You and Michael have stood by me," his voice quavered slightly. "It means more than you could ever know." He looked at the door.

George appeared in the doorway and immediately rushed to embrace his uncle.

"And this guy," he said as they hugged once more.

~ ~ ~

Monday morning Hope surprised herself by not rushing to school. Though she arose early—even on these days when school was out for the summer, today she took time for a leisurely breakfast. Instead of reading the newspaper, she relived the day before and enjoyed Theo's delightful response to the much-anticipated Item#247.

For some time, she had been unable to recover from his implication that because of her having siphoned money from Mary Baldwin's account, she was still a felon, albeit an unindicted one.

This single remark had festered away for months and exacerbated the acute guilt she lived with daily.

He, on the other hand, was a convicted felon from his brush with the Dixie Mafia in his young years. But having served his time in prison, he had paid his debt to society, he insisted.

Hope had never come to terms with the hurtful context in which Theo had compared their situations. It was too painful to recall.

But now things had changed. Theo deserved her trust. His response to Item#247 convinced her he was in her corner.

"That is brilliant news, Hope. I knew there was no possible way you could have been an actual felon," he had said with obvious warmth and sincerity, hugging her tightly.

Only Theo could manage the perfect comment to erase the doubt she had harbored about trusting his underlying judgment of her. She instantly forgave him for having said the dreaded f-word.

More importantly, he had erased the self-doubt which had haunted her since the night of her confession to him when he had offensively referred to her as a *felon*.

Of course she well deserved Mary Baldwin's support and protection too.

Or did she?

~ ~ ~

Pulling into the lot at Poore Pond School, Hope was taken aback by the sight of Ray Sellers' van. Her breath stopped. He was not supposed to be on the premises as long as his case was pending. Was he here to deliver more terrible news?

"Look who's here, Dr. Fleming," Corinne chirped, nodding toward the open door of Hope's inner office.

Looking rested and fit, Ray approached her and offered his hand. He was dressed in his blue work shirt.

"Ray," she said, shaking his hand vigorously and returning his smile. "You have good news written all over you. What's happened?"

"The best possible thing," he said, taking the chair Hope gestured him toward.

"Did you settle out of court?" she asked.

"Even better, Hope." Ray's face grew serious. "Tommy—that poor kid—confessed that he had made up the entire story. All of it."

"Whatever prompted him to retract his story, Ray?"

"My attorney Fiona Fitzenrider; you've met her, Hope," he said.

"Yes I have. At your wedding reception, right? Attractive redhead?"

"Right, not the kind of woman you'd forget," Ray chortled.

"Indeed," Hope said, recalling images of the curvy Fiona in a sexy red cocktail suit, flirting for all the world with Theo. "What did the clever Fiona manage to do?"

"She had an informal meeting with Tommy's father at his house, and Tommy overheard everything," Ray explained.

"Overheard what?" she said as Corinne walked in with two coffees.

"Thank you, Corinne," they said in unison.

"Tommy overheard Fiona blasting Grant with strong words, throwing up his failures as a husband and a father. She accused him of not really wanting to be a father, and on and on. It wasn't pretty," Ray said, dropping his eyes.

"Tommy overheard all that about his father and was moved to come clean?" Hope asked.

"That's about the size of it," he said.

Ray shook his head slowly. "All this has been hard on the boy."

Hope stared at him. "Not half as hard as sticking to those false accusations would have been, Ray."

"I know that," he said.

"Do we know his motive?"

"Well, the child psychologist's opinion was that the school vandalism was out of character for Tommy. She was able to get him to talk about his poor relationship with the stepmother who kept riding him about being a bum, taunting him that he would never amount to anything." Ray said, looking at her with sad eyes.

"The psychologist—what was her name?" Hope asked.

Ray shuffled in the chair. "I'm not sure, Dr. Stinson or Stinton, something like that," he murmured.

"So Dr. Stinson or Stinton's impression was that Tommy made a poor choice to vandalize the school then when he realized he would get into trouble with the law, he accused you of unspeakable deeds to—what? Give himself an out?" she said falteringly.

"I guess to get the focus off his being a criminal and onto his being a victim," Ray said, frowning. "Maybe work it for a little sympathy."

"Tommy had a good record here, for the most part," Hope said. "But we did get wind of some behavioral problems at the middle school last fall. Was that about the time Stepmother came on the scene?"

"I believe so," he said. "The doctor called it *inverse motivation* or something like that."

"Children today are certainly aware of their power to cause great damage by making insidious accusations of sexual violations," Hope said, looking at the courtyard. "They learn it from the news, from television and movie drama, sometimes from actual events in their own families."

"Well, Tommy had a personal tutor on the subject, someone who had used the tactic twice," Ray said.

"And who might that have been, Ray?" she asked.

"Josh, Josh Wentworth. You remember, the boy who did not attend Poore Pond; he was with Tommy and Andrew when I found them in the field that night."

Ray went on to tell Josh's story, including the fact that though the coach he had accused of molesting him was found innocent, his reputation was forever clouded.

The same was true of the step-grandfather with the coin collection. The courts believed in his innocence, but some members of his own family feared him as a lecherous predator and saw that their small children were never alone with him.

Stunned by these disclosures and filled with joy for Ray and his family, Hope's emotions approached overload. She stood and stretched her shoulders.

"I see you're wearing your work shirt, Ray," she smiled.

"I know; I really missed wearing it, guess I was fantasizing about being back at work," he said sheepishly.

They talked about procedures the school board would need to follow before he could return to his job and estimated that he should be back in a matter of weeks.

Corinne gave him an affectionate goodbye, and Hope walked him to the main entrance.

"We're anxious to have you back, Ray," she said, shaking his hand warmly. "It may be a little awkward at first but nothing you can't handle."

"I'm anxious to come back, Hope," he said softly, his eyes wandering down the hall, filled with overflowing trash cans outside classroom doors. Why didn't Maynor ask the kids to empty those cans on the last day of school, he wondered. They love that job, especially on the last day when they are so antsy for summer break to start.

"What's the latest with Caroline, Ray?" Hope asked with kind eyes. "Will she be released anytime soon?"

"No one seems to know," Ray said in a thick voice; he looked sadly into space.

"Claire and Leonard—they're a twosome now," he said, needing to change the subject.

"Did I hear they were engaged?" Hope asked.

"Sort of, well, yes," he said, meeting Hope's gaze.

"Sort of?" she asked.

"Well, it's just that Claire doesn't want Mom to be upset. She thinks Claire hasn't known him long enough to be sure." He spread his palms, emphasizing his point. "Heck, she's right."

"What were you saying about Caroline's release, Ray?"

"The doctors won't release Mom until she's able to stand on her own. The therapy she's getting at the rehab center is supposed to be strengthening her legs, but—." He stared out the window.

"Is it having any effect at all, Ray?" Hope asked, lifting the contents from her inbox.

He shook his head, disheartened eyes meeting hers. Unspoken words of the possibility that Caroline may never come home hung palpably in the air.

"We'll see you soon, Ray," she said as they hugged awkwardly at the door.

Hope felt restless and unsettled. She toured the building, checking to see how Joe was doing with year-end tasks.

She discovered him taking apart a math bulletin board in Chuck Taylor's room.

"Joe, how did you get stuck with this job?" she asked.

"I signed the volunteer sheet to help Mr. Taylor while he's recuperating."

They discussed Ray's imminent return. Joe told Hope he was bidding on a job opening back at the high school. "These little ones are much more enjoyable, but there's too much liability at the elementary level." He looked down, kicking at a spot of dried paste on the floor.

"I know, Joe," Hope said warmly.

"I cannot tell you how relieved I was when Julian's parents decided not to sue." He coughed into his sleeve.

"Weren't we all? But I must say, schools tend not to be held liable for such things unless blatant neglect can be proven." She smiled at him. "The court's definition of *negligence* is 'failure to exercise ordinary prudence.' The children were not unsupervised, Joe; you were standing right there."

"I know, but…" His face filled with distress.

Hope could see the emotion he was trying so hard to mask. "It's time to stop beating yourself up about that incident. Julian has recovered very well."

He resumed removing paper cutouts from Chuck's bulletin board. Hope gathered the spent staples.

"You'll be pleased to hear that Chuck is volunteering for a cyber-bullying hotline," she said.

Joe turned toward her. "I heard about that. I understand he'll be working from home, using his computer. That's great."

Hope dropped the pile of staples in a waste can and offered her hand to Joe. They shook hands warmly and wished one another good luck.

Back in the office, Hope took the letter Corinne handed her. An official-looking, heavy linen envelope bore a federal seal on the flap. She stared at the seal.

"Chuck Taylor called, Hope," Corinne said while sorting papers on her desk into neat piles. "He wanted me to tell you that he is withdrawing his suit for divorce."

"Really?" Hope asked, surprised. She lifted her eyes from the imposing envelope. "Did he say what caused his change of heart?"

Corinne pulled her handbag from a desk drawer and walked to Hope. "He didn't say much." She swallowed and lowered her eyes. "But he did manage to tell me that the courts have found

Felice mentally incompetent."

She grasped Hope's outstretched hand and their eyes met. "He was so choked up he was barely able to blurt out a good-bye."

They hugged warmly, and Hope watched Corinne go down the hall.

She hurried into the private office. Her heart quickened as she slid the letter opener under the flap.

Dr. Hope Minster Fleming, the engraved announcement read with great authority.

Congratulations.

You have been invited

to audition for appointment to the

United States

Department of Education Task Force:

Creating World Class Schools

under the direction of

Education Secretary William Wertheimer

Hope noted the Secretary's name and gasped. Her mind raced. Out of the blue like this? William Wertheimer has never met me. What makes him think I might be qualified?

She thought for one mad moment she might call the Education Secretary then realized she did not have a phone number. But Bernard surely has it. Bernard.

This is his doing. Of course.

Hope sat back and closed her eyes, imagining herself on the task force. She thought of Mary Baldwin. *I loved her like a daughter and found immense personal joy in her successes.*

"Mary would be so proud of me," she whispered as she tucked the thick card into its envelope and slipped it into her purse.

~ ~ ~

At dinner that evening, Theo proposed a toast to Hope for the illustrious honor bestowed upon her by Secretary of Education, Mr. Wertheimer.

They clinked their wine glasses together.

"Well, Hope," Theo said smilingly. "What are your thoughts in regard to swimming with the big fish on this task force?"

"You don't mean the sharks, do you, Theo?" she asked with furrowed brow.

"You could say that, couldn't you," Theo chuckled and raised his brows at her.

Noting a fleeting look of fear in her eyes, he quickly said, "Just joking of course."

"It is important to remember," she said, composing herself, "that this is not an appointment, Theo. It is merely an *invitation to audition for appointment.*"

Suddenly they both broke bits of bread, making a long, slow job of dipping it into seasoned oil. The small act seemed to require utmost concentration and silence.

Threads of doubt began to form in Hope's mind. I cannot possibly be qualified for this appointment, she told herself. How have I distinguished myself? I haven't. I should disqualify myself and avoid the humiliation of rejection.

"I will not delude myself," she said. "I have been too busy managing a school to find time to distinguish myself in community service." She opened the napkin in the silver bread bowl but found it empty.

Theo signaled the waiter to bring more.

"How soon may we expect our dinners?" he asked when the waiter returned with fresh bread.

The waiter apologized and hurried away.

"Mark my word, Hope," Theo said, knowing her propensity for self-doubt. "Everyone invited to audition will end up being appointed.This so-called *audition* is just s process to ensure that all candidates use the language correctly and have a professional appearance—no cowboy types or two-headed freaks allowed."

Their dinners arrived on steaming plates.

"That looks luscious," Hope said, grateful for a change of subject. She managed to avoid further discussion of the task force by updating Theo on all those who had stopped in at Poore Pond that day.

"The way you are such a large part of the lives of everyone on your staff, Hope, never fails to astound me,"Theo said, shaking his head.

"Are you calling me a busybody,Theo?" Hope laughed.

"Not at all; I think it's wonderful," he said.

"Do you know what else is wonderful? The way Mark has forged ahead with the grant applications. He has already submitted three of them and did a masterful job of keeping the tone very unlawyerly—quite full of humanitarian points in clear, straightforward language."

"That's great," she said. "I am sure he will get the grantors' attention for us."

They discussed dessert and agreed to share a decadent double-chocolate brownie with ice cream.

Theo sat back in his chair and smoothed his napkin."You know, Hope, you and George should be proud of The George Fleming Shelter you've established so successfully—in fact, founding a homeless shelter is community service *par excellence*."

"Do you really think so,Theo?" she asked, her eyes glistening. with pleasure.

"Of course," he said."Let's drink to your benefactor, Hope. She must be pleased with you too; her wings are fairly bursting with pride, I'm sure."They raised their glasses and looked heavenward.

Hope drained her glass and sat back. She felt a glimmer of redemption that allowed her—for the first time—a moment of self-esteem. She was struck by the heady effect of feeling good about herself.

She vowed to hold onto this sense of redemption, the notion that she could be a better person. I must not miss a single opportunity to reach out with human kindness to everyone I encounter.

> *"For by grace are ye saved through faith:*
> *and that not of yourselves: it is the gift of God."*
> *Ephesians 2:8*

Reference Notes

Chapter 4 1. *Court Rulings Are Vague on School Dress Codes,* Armond Budish, The Plain Dealer, Cleveland, Ohio (September 22, 2002) p.C-6

2. *Phonics, Syllable and Accent Rules,* http://English. glendale.cc.ca.us/phonics.rules.html (November 18, 2008)

Chapter 7 3. *Dixie Mafia's Locales and MO, The Early Days,* http://en.wikipedia.org/wiki/Dixie_Mafia (November 20, 2008)

Chapter 8 4. Muscle *Atrophy,* Helio Health Library, http://www. healiohealth.com/muscle-atrophy-treatment.html (February 18, 2009)

Chapter 9 5. *No Child Left Behind Act,* Wikipedia, http:// en.wikipedia.org/wike/No_Child_Left_Behind_Act (October 18, 2011)

6. *Munchausen by Proxy Syndrome,* http://home. coqui.net/myrna/munch.htm (July 26, 2005)

Chapter 13 7. *10 Steps to World-Class American Schools,* William Brock, Ray Marshall, Marc Tucker, The Plain Dealer, Cleveland, Ohio (June 7, 2009), p. G-6

8. *Traction,* Tish Davidson The Gale Group, Inc., http://www.healthline.com/galecontent/traction (October 17, 2011)

Chapter 16 9. *Child's Death Leads to Safer School Policy,* Harlan Spector, The Plain Dealer, Cleveland, Ohio (July 10, 2007), p.B-1

Chapter 18 10. *Munchausen Syndrome by Proxy,* Copyright 1995-2008 The Cleveland Clinic Foundation, provided to Wikipedia, http://en.wickipedia.org/Munchausen_syndrome_byproxy (October 20, 2009)

Chapter 19 11. *The Emperor Has No Clothes,* PHONICS TALK: Volume 35 (May, 2009) by Dolores G. Hiskes, with excerpt from *New York Times* article (June 3, 1999), http://www.nrrf/PhonicsTalk_vol35_May09.htm (October 28, 2009)

Chapter 24 12. See note 10 above.

Discussion

1. Hope Fleming's discomfort with Mark Fleming's portrayal of his brother Michael as helpful, unselfish, caring is clear. What events support Mark's opinion?

2. Theodore Keller discloses his past as a felon due to involvement with the Dixie Mafia. To what extent does Hope identify with Theo? For what reasons?

3. How worthwhile are Hope's efforts to emphasize the correct usage of articles *a, an, the*, preceding words beginning with vowels? Should sublime speech matter?

4. Hope involves herself in Chuck and Felice Taylor's personal conflicts. Does she overstep? How would you, as principal, have handled the situation?

5. Ray Sellers is unjustly accused by a student, of sexual molestation. What important truths can be derived from the entire incident?

6. Both teacher Bluewave Stonecipher and attorney Fiona Fitzenrider mention the adage, *It's there inside you,* to Ray. Discuss what it apparently means in the mind of each woman.

7. Ray visits student Julian Barrett, recovering at home from a cafeteria accident. Was that appropriate behavior for a head custodian under these circumstances? Under any circumstances?

8. At the faculty meeting, teacher Katrina Davis presses Dr. Hope for her views on merit pay for teachers by asking specific questions: "Are you in favor of it? If so, what are the pros? If so, how do you see it working procedurally? If so, should it apply to principals as well?" How did Hope handle Katrina's concerns? What do you think about this timely matter?

9. What does Hope's term the *Baldwin Curse* say about her view of the new information she has concerning Mary Baldwin's regard for her?

10. The Poore Pond novels are in large part about relationships. Human relationships are dynamic in that they are constantly changing. Which characters' relationships were most interesting to you and why?

About The Author

Ruth Harwell Fawcett is a retired educator turned writer, publisher, and consultant. She writes about her favorite place to be—a school. Dr. Fawcett left her place in education earlier than planned in order to live her writing dream. Having become a published writer, she is now leading other writers toward their writing visions. *Honor and Grace* is the third novel in the Poore Pond School trilogy.

Ruth lives with her husband and son, dividing her time between Cleveland and Atlanta where her two daughters reside with their husbands and their offspring—and in some cases, their offspring—all providing more fodder for fictional characters.

The Cover Artist

Pamela Dills, cover artist for the Poore Pond Series, has had a diverse career in the field of art. She earned a BFA from Kent State University and began her career as a graphic artist in Washington, D.C., with an advertising firm. She continued in advertising in Cleveland, directing major and varied accounts.

After a sabbatical to raise her two sons, she has returned to her field as a free-lance artist specializing in acrylics and pastels. She shows her work in galleries throughout Cleveland and southern Florida.

Pamela lives in Cleveland with her husband and three dogs.